URBAN
OUTLAWS
SHOCKWAVE

PETER JAY BLACK

BLOOMSBURY

LONDON OXFORD NEW YORK NEW DELHI SYDNEY

Bloomsbury Publishing, London, Oxford, New York, New Delhi and Sydney

First published in Great Britain in November 2016 by Bloomsbury Publishing Plc
50 Bedford Square, London WC1B 3DP

www.bloomsbury.com

BLOOMSBURY is a registered trademark of Bloomsbury Publishing Plc

A CIP catalogue record for this book is available from the British Library

ISBN 978 1 4088 5151 7

Typeset by Integra Software Services Pvt. Ltd.
Printed and bound in Great Britain by CPI Group (UK) Ltd, Croydon CR0 4YY

1 3 5 7 9 10 8 6 4 2

Dedicated to you, the reader

CHAPTER ONE

JACK FENTON STOOD IN THE DARKNESS, HIS EARS ringing from the explosion and his body shaking. For the first time in his life, he felt real, uncontrollable panic.

His brain refused to function properly – he just remained still, like an idiot, thoughts frozen.

The crackling sound of boots on shattered concrete came from somewhere ahead. Jack's ears strained to locate the sound and he guessed it must be one of the armed men stepping over the bunker's airlock door – the one they'd just blown from its hinges.

A light appeared behind Jack, partly illuminating the corridor. Dazed, he turned to look at it.

Charlie stood in the doorway to her workshop, holding a small torch in her trembling hand. 'Jack?' she whispered, her eyes fearful. 'We've got to get out of here.'

He stared at her.

Get out?

No, what he needed to do was wake up.

How had he got them into this nightmare – the five Urban Outlaws against a group of men with guns and explosives?

Jack gasped at the thought. *Where are the others? Are any of them hurt?*

Charlie stood beside him. 'Jack?' she breathed in his ear. 'What are you doing? We need to move.'

Jack took the torch from her, edged around the corner and peered down the next hallway.

It was filled with thick smoke and the torchlight only penetrated a couple of metres.

Jack glanced at Charlie again, unsure what to do. *Why can't I think straight?*

Charlie pulled her bandana up, covering her nose and mouth, and whispered, 'Is something on fire?'

'I don't know,' Jack murmured.

Maybe it was to do with the explosion or perhaps it was smoke grenades. He couldn't tell, and that was because at that moment he just felt stunned.

Jack turned back in the direction of the main bunker and tried to focus.

What's the matter with you? he thought. *Figure it out, and fast. Otherwise we're all dead.*

The men Hector had hired to raid the place were obviously professionals. Common thugs would be barking out commands by now, revealing their whereabouts.

These guys were silent, which made Jack's blood run cold.

His ears strained to pick up any other movement and he wondered if they had heat-vision goggles, able to cut through the dark and the smoke.

Body tensed, he edged forward as quietly as he could, one foot in front of the other, with Charlie following close behind. Somehow, they needed to get to the other Outlaws.

They'd just reached the end of the corridor when Jack heard the faint sound of more boot-clad footsteps.

Measured.

Precise.

They're definitely coming in, he thought.

Panic tore through Jack as ahead of him, through the smoke, faint lights and shadows moved. The men were fanning out and methodically searching the room.

A torch beam swept in their direction and instinct kicked in. Jack leapt backwards, pulling Charlie with him, and held his breath.

If there was just a way to –

Hands grabbed Jack's shoulders, yanking him sideways. He struggled to fight them off but someone hissed in his ear, 'It's me.'

Slink pulled Jack and Charlie into the generator room, closed the door silently behind them and bolted it.

An emergency light bathed the generators, pipework and concrete walls in a muted red.

'As soon as I saw them on the CCTV,' Slink said in a hurried whisper, 'I ran in here and cut the power.'

Jack let out a breath. 'Good work.'

Thank God *someone* had reacted fast.

'Then I heard the explosion.' Slink looked at the door, his eyes reflecting Jack's concern.

'Where are Wren and Obi?' Jack asked, fearful of what the answer might be.

'Wren's following the emergency escape plan.' Slink thrust a thumb over his shoulder.

In the corner of the generator room was a large vertical cylinder. It was the main duct that dragged air from the surface. Its access panel was open, and

Jack could see the metal ladder mounted to the inner wall.

'What about Obi?' Jack asked.

Slink looked at the floor and sighed. 'He was in his chair. I was so determined to grab Wren and cut the power that there ... there just wasn't enough time to get him.' He looked up at them. 'And then I couldn't go back without being spotted.'

Charlie rested a hand on his shoulder. 'You did brilliantly. If it wasn't for you, we'd all have been caught by now.'

Slink shrugged. 'Maybe. So, what now?'

Jack looked at Slink's ankle – he'd sprained it just before the Facility mission. Slink said it was healing nicely but he still limped when he walked, and that, coupled with the virus, meant Slink wasn't on top form.

Jack gestured to the air vent. 'You go first.'

Slink didn't move.

'Go,' Jack insisted. 'Please.'

With Jack and Charlie's help, Slink reluctantly climbed into the vent and disappeared up the ladder.

'What about Obi?' Charlie asked.

'I'm going back for him.'

'*What?*' Charlie said. 'You can't. They'll get you.'

'I have to try.'

'I'm coming with you.'

'No,' Jack said. 'That'll double our chances of getting caught.' He gestured to the ladder. 'Meet us at the top.'

Charlie hesitated.

'Please, Charlie,' Jack said urgently. 'We're wasting time.'

Charlie's shoulders slumped. 'Fine. But be careful, OK?'

'Sure.'

Jack helped her inside and as soon as she was safely on the ladder, he ran to the door, pulled back the bolt and slowly turned the handle.

Jack peered into the hallway and, seeing lights still coming from the main bunker, he slipped out and sprinted in the opposite direction.

As he ran, Jack switched on Charlie's torch and cupped it in his hand, allowing just enough light to see a metre or so ahead.

His body ached, which made running hard, but Jack found the next hallway and peered around the corner. It was empty. He hurried to the end, went right and then darted into Obi's bedroom.

Jack's heart sank.

Obi wasn't there.

Jack rushed to the other door, which led back to the main bunker, opened it a crack and peered through.

In the gloom, he could just make out Obi. He was sitting perfectly still in his modified dentist's chair, shielded from the torchlight by the darkened screens of his computers.

Jack glanced about. He had to get Obi's attention without alerting the men.

He spotted Obi's mechanical grabber on the table by the door, scooped it up and peered into the bunker.

Several torch beams swept the room. The men were checking under furniture and were being careful to stay in sight of one another, fanning out and blocking what they thought was the only exit.

Jack looked back at Obi and reached out with the grabber. He was about to tap him on the shoulder when Obi let out a giant sneeze that made Jack almost leap out of his skin.

A torch beam flashed in their direction.

'*There*,' a deep voice snapped.

A pair of hands grabbed Obi and he cried out.

Jack spun around, sprinted through Obi's bedroom and back into the corridor, the sound of a pair of heavy boots in hot pursuit.

'Stop!'

Jack ran up the hallway and took a sharp left. His feet almost tripped over one another, but somehow he managed to stay upright and keep going.

He heard the man slide around the corner and slam into the wall behind him.

Not looking back, Jack took another left and shouldered open the door to the generator room. He slammed it shut just as a body crashed into it from the other side.

Jack threw the bolt across and stepped back, wheezing and feeling tight-chested.

Obi.

He'd failed.

'One of the kids just went in there,' a voice said.

There was the sound of hurried footfalls then a motor whirred.

Jack took another step back as sparks flew.

They were grinding off the door's hinges.

He hesitated, desperately trying to think of another way to get to Obi, but there was no way for him to make it back to the main bunker without being caught, and the other Outlaws needed him, especially now they were all ill.

Realising there was nothing more he could do, Jack muttered, 'I'm sorry.' With a heavy heart, he hurried to the air duct and climbed in.

Air rushed past him, dragged down by a large fan beneath his feet. Jack scrambled up the ladder as fast as his aching limbs allowed.

Finally, above his head, the duct tapered, becoming too narrow for him to fit in. He turned around and squeezed through another opening.

Once out of the air duct, he glanced down the shaft in time to see a man wearing a gas mask step on to the ladder. He had a rifle slung over his shoulder.

Jack turned back. He was now in a small room with no windows or doors. Ahead of him, low to the floor, was a thick concrete sewer pipe, two metres in diameter, with a section of its wall removed.

Charlie was loading a cart into it. It was one of her own creations – the cart looked like an oversized skateboard with a large electric motor on the back, a padded seat and several batteries.

Two other identical carts rested against the wall.

'What happened?' Charlie looked pale in the artificial light.

'Hurry,' Jack urged her. 'I'll explain later.'

Charlie climbed on to the cart and lay down. 'See you there.' She pressed a button on the hand control and zoomed off down the pipe.

Jack grabbed one of the remaining carts.

The ladder in the air duct rattled.

If he hadn't been so stupid – so slow to come up with a plan – he would've got Obi out of there and they'd both be making their escape with the rest of the Outlaws.

Swearing under his breath, Jack lifted the cart into the pipe and climbed on. He clutched the hand control and flipped a switch. A spotlight came on between his feet, illuminating the tunnel ahead.

'Stop right there.' The masked man climbed down from the air duct and swung his gun from his shoulder.

Jack pressed another button on the control and his head was thrown back as the electric cart shot down the pipe at blistering speed.

And that was the moment Jack seriously regretted what he was doing – as his cheeks rippled with the force of the air, and his eyes streamed, he remembered there was no way to slow the cart down. The second he'd pressed that button, there was no going back because it was automatic.

Jack managed to lift his head a few millimetres, blinked away the tears and peered forwards. The lamplight showed nothing but a black hole ahead of him, as if he was hurtling towards the centre of the Earth.

For a couple of hundred metres the pipe remained straight and the cart continued to accelerate, gaining speed with every second, making it hard for Jack to keep his head up.

The electric motor emitted a high-pitched whirring sound and the rubber wheels buzzed and smoked.

Suddenly the pipe snapped to the right, almost throwing Jack off. Then it made a sweeping left turn and straightened up.

Jack closed his eyes briefly and prayed he made it to the end in one piece.

The pipe rose up a steep incline then dropped down, like a crazy roller coaster. Jack held on tight.

As impossible as it seemed, the cart continued to speed up, and for a split second Jack imagined what would happen if its wheels came off.

The pipe went into a tight corkscrew with the cart shooting up the sides of the spiral. Then, mercifully, it straightened out again.

Jack took deep breaths, trying not to throw up.

He heard a buzzing noise behind him and managed to turn his head enough to see that the masked man was on the third cart and seemed, incredibly, to be gaining on him.

Jack looked forwards as the pipe went up a short incline then took a sharp right and another.

He tried to remember how much further it was. Whatever happened, he couldn't let the masked man either catch up with him or reach the end.

As Jack's cart continued to follow the twists and turns of the pipe, he wriggled out of his hoodie, pulled it over his head and clutched it to his chest.

The pipe straightened and he glanced back. The masked man was only a few metres away.

Jack threw his hoodie behind him and watched as it got caught in the pursuing cart's wheels, flipping it forward and slamming the masked man's head into the pipe's ceiling.

Jack winced and turned around.

His cart went up another hill then right, and started to slow down.

Jack loosened his grip and tried to bring his breathing under control. Sweat soaked his clothes and stung his eyes.

Finally, the pipe opened and the cart slid to a halt.

Charlie held out a hand and pulled Jack to his feet.

He wobbled for a second and took a moment to regain his balance. 'We had company,' he wheezed, gesturing down the pipe.

Charlie's eyes widened. 'One of them followed us?'

'Yeah, but I took care of it.' Jack glanced around the room. 'Where are the others?'

'They'll be heading to the rendezvous point,' Charlie said. 'Following the escape plan.'

'Good.' Jack straightened up. 'Come on.'

'What about Obi?' Charlie asked.

Jack cringed inside and a wave of guilt washed over him. 'I'll explain once we're back with Slink and Wren.'

Together, they hurried to the door.

On the other side was a set of concrete steps, and Jack and Charlie bounded up them.

At the top, they stopped at a moss-covered wall. At least it looked like a wall. As with a lot of places in London, appearances were deceptive.

Charlie looked at Jack. 'Ready?'

He took a breath and nodded.

Together they shouldered the wall and it slowly swung open. They kept pushing until there was a gap big enough for them to slip through.

Charlie went first and Jack followed.

In front of them was the Tower of London. It looked foreboding with its high stone walls and turrets lit up against a darkened sky.

Jack glanced around. Directly above their heads was a security camera – a modern addition.

'This way,' he said, jogging to their right.

A scraping noise made Jack spin back towards the secret door and his eyes went wide as he saw the masked man stagger out of it, his clothes torn and his face covered in blood.

'You have got to be kidding me,' Jack said, hardly believing his eyes.

'I thought you said you took care of him?' Charlie turned and ran.

Jack raced after her. 'I thought I did.'

They sprinted up a ramp and vaulted a low wall.

Tourists jumped clear as the Outlaws shoved their way past.

'Hey!'

'What's your game?'

Jack looked over his shoulder. The man was giving chase, his twisted features expressing pure rage.

Keeping their heads low, Jack and Charlie sprinted along a narrow street, weaving between sightseers.

'How far?' Jack shouted.

The escape plan said they were supposed to be going the opposite way, but Charlie had obviously decided on a different destination.

'Half a mile,' she called back as she squeezed past an elderly couple.

'You've got to be winding me up.' Jack's lungs burnt, and his body felt almost out of energy.

'Come on,' Charlie shouted.

Jack glanced back again. Now the man had a phone pressed to his ear and was barking commands as he ran after them.

Charlie darted across the road, and a taxi slammed on its brakes and beeped its horn.

Without stopping, Jack followed her up another street, dashing between traffic and pedestrians.

Just as Jack felt he couldn't run any further, he looked back to see their pursuer slowing down, clutching his side and staring intently at them.

Ahead, horns blared as two black minivans drove up the street the wrong way.

'Charlie?'

'What?'

He pointed.

Several men dressed in military uniform climbed out of each van.

Charlie swore and darted right, sprinting up another road.

Jack groaned and raced after her.

At the end, they took a left.

'Are we running in circles?' Jack shouted.

'Not exactly,' Charlie called over her shoulder.

'Great.' Jack risked another backward glance and saw that the bad guys were still following.

'This way.' Charlie sprinted down an alleyway.

When they emerged on the other side, Tower Hill Underground station loomed before them. It was packed with commuters coming and going.

Jack cringed, thinking of the virus he would spread among them with every panting breath.

'Find another way,' he shouted at Charlie.

Two minivans screeched to a halt to their left and more armed men climbed out.

'No choice,' Charlie shouted back.

They launched themselves through the station's entrance and down the steps.

Four men gave chase.

'They're not giving up,' Jack called to Charlie.

They pushed through the crowds and vaulted the barriers.

The men behind did the same, shoving people out of the way as they went.

Jack and Charlie ran on to the platform just as the train's doors started to close. They both dived through the carriage at the same time and crumpled on to the floor.

Jack rolled on to his back and looked up. One of the men glared through the window as the train pulled away from the platform.

Breathing hard and clutching his chest, Jack got to his feet and helped Charlie up.

An old woman frowned at them.

Jack offered her a weak smile. 'Late for school.'

The woman's frown deepened. 'It's quarter to six.'

'Evening classes.'

Charlie grabbed Jack's arm and pulled him to a seat in the emptiest corner of the carriage. She lifted her bandana up over her nose and mouth.

Jack pulled his shirt up over the lower half of his face. He knew they had to keep as far away from people as they could for fear of infecting them, but things hadn't exactly gone to plan so far.

Another wave of guilt washed over Jack, and his thoughts drifted back to the last conversation they'd had with Hector – when Hector had revealed that not only had he tricked the Outlaws into unleashing a deadly virus, but that his father, Benito Del Sarto, had woken up from a coma and divulged their bunker's location.

The bunker had been a secret since before any of the Outlaws were born, the location known to only a few people during its decades of existence. For a fleeting moment, Jack imagined the shame of having to tell Noble that it was his fault they'd lost it.

Cold horror washed over him as he realised that this wasn't just another petty fight – Hector was making a final push to destroy the Outlaws once and for all.

'I have to go back,' Jack muttered.

Charlie stared at him. 'Go back?'

'Obi. I have to do something. Maybe I can follow them when they come out.'

'They'll kill you.'

'They'll kill Obi.'

'No they won't,' Charlie hissed.

Jack frowned at her. 'What do you mean?'

'Hector will use Obi as insurance.'

'Insurance?'

'Think about it, Jack,' Charlie said, glancing around the carriage and lowering her voice further. 'They caught Obi but no one else, so what will they do now? What is Hector's next move going to be when he finds out the rest of us managed to escape?'

Jack stared at her as scenarios ran through his head. If they only captured Obi then Hector would use him as bait to round up the others.

Jack rubbed his aching leg muscles. 'We could be making a huge mistake here, Charlie.'

She let out a breath and stared at the floor. 'We can't do anything for Obi right now. He needs us to get away so we can save him later.'

Jack had to admit that Charlie was right.

He sighed. 'Have you got your phone on you?'

'No.'

'Me neither. Any cash?'

Charlie shook her head.

'Brilliant.' Jack stared at the floor too.

Not only had they just lost their home and Obi, but they had no money or any form of communication – and it was all his fault.

*

Jack and Charlie marched around the lake in St James's Park.

It was dark and luckily there was no one else around – Jack didn't want to infect even more people. God only knew how many they'd given the virus to already and he cringed as he thought of all those passengers on the Underground.

As they crossed over a low concrete bridge, he could see Buckingham Palace in one direction and Horse Guards Parade and the London Eye in the other.

In the middle of the bridge, Slink and Wren were waiting for them.

'Where's Obi?' Slink said, leaning against the metal railing to take the weight off his ankle.

'I couldn't get to him,' Jack said in a low voice, his face burning with shame.

Wren's eyes filled with tears. 'Will they hurt him?'

'No,' Charlie said, taking her hands. 'He'll be fine. We just need to stay strong and find out where Hector takes him, then we'll break him out again. Yeah?'

Wren sniffed and nodded.

A guy walking a golden retriever started to cross the bridge towards them.

'Come on,' Jack said, gesturing for the others to follow him.

They needed to stay away from other people, but without the bunker to retreat to that was going to be extremely difficult.

Once he felt they were a safe distance away, under the cover of trees, Jack stopped and turned back to the three of them.

'So,' Slink said, looking puzzled by Jack's actions. 'Are you gonna tell us what's going on or what?'

Jack cleared his throat and started to bring Slink and Wren up to speed. He told them how Hector had caught Cloud feeding information to the Outlaws, how he'd sent his team to the Facility a couple of days before the Outlaws had broken in themselves. How Hector had shown his father awake from the coma that had kept their bunker safe for so long. Lastly, Jack told Slink and Wren about Medusa, the virus, and how they were all infected now.

'A virus?' Slink stared at him. 'Are you kidding?'

'No,' Jack said. 'You know that rash we all have behind our ears? Hector said that's the first sign of the virus.'

'I thought we just had bad colds,' Wren said in a small voice.

Jack shook his head. 'Hector says that we brought it out of the Facility and we've infected loads of people by now.' He glanced around to make sure no one else was about before continuing, 'We all need to keep as far away from other people as possible.'

'So there *was* a weapon in the Facility?' Wren asked.

Jack sighed and nodded.

Slink frowned. 'Wait a minute. You can't be serious, Jack.'

Jack nodded again, even though he wished none of it was true.

Slink kept his voice low. 'How bad is it?'

'Bad.' Jack shrugged. 'A week. Maybe two. I just don't know how long before...'

'What's he on about?' Slink said, glancing at Charlie. 'Before what?'

'Before we're, you know, *done for*,' Charlie said.

Wren gasped. 'We're going to die?'

Slink's eyes widened. 'This can't be happening.'

'I wish I could tell you it wasn't,' Jack said. 'But it explains why we all feel rubbish, why we have the rash.'

'I thought we caught it off Raze,' Slink said, dumbfounded and staring into the distance. 'Thought we had that bozo's germs.'

'That's what we all thought,' Charlie said. 'But it's Medusa, and it's just going to get worse.'

Slink lunged for Jack's throat.

'*Slink.*' Charlie grabbed hold of Slink and tried to pull him off, but he had a tight grip.

Slink squeezed Jack's neck hard. 'I'm gonna kill you,' he screamed.

CHAPTER TWO

JACK STRUGGLED TO BREATHE AS SLINK'S HAND tightened around his throat.

'Slink, stop it,' Wren cried out.

Charlie wrestled with him, but Slink was too strong and he gripped Jack's throat harder, apparently determined to crush the life from him.

Jack twisted his body, grabbed Slink's wrists and, with supreme effort, finally managed to shove him off.

Charlie took hold of him. 'Calm down, Slink.'

Slink thrashed about, trying to break free, but she bear-hugged him and pinned his arms to his sides.

'Get off me.'

'I said, calm down,' Charlie snapped.

'No. You're a moron,' Slink snarled at Jack.

Jack stared back at him, unsure what to do.

Slink broke from Charlie's grasp and took a swipe at Jack, missing by millimetres. 'We should be in quarantine or something.'

'Slink.' Charlie grabbed hold of him again.

Jack knew Slink was right and he felt terrible about it. In a way, he wished Charlie would just let Slink punch him. Perhaps that would make them both feel better.

Charlie took Slink's shoulders and turned him around to face her. 'Listen.'

'Get off me, Charlie.' Slink glared over her shoulder at Jack.

'Not until you listen,' Charlie said, shaking him.

'I'm done listening.'

'No, you're not.'

'Slink,' Wren said in a calming voice. 'It's not Jack's fault. It's Hector. Hector did this.'

Slink didn't take his eyes off Jack, but he did visibly relax – just a little.

Charlie seized her chance. 'Just think about it a minute,' she said, looking at him intently. 'We've all had the virus for a few days now. There was no way for any of us to know that. Yes, we've passed it on to other people, but that's not our fault or Jack's. We were tricked by Hector.'

'We're always being tricked by Hector,' Slink spat. He waved a finger at Jack. 'And we're always the ones getting caught up in your stupid war with him. Now look what's happened. Are you happy? Huh, Jack? We're going to die because of you. How does *that* make you feel?'

. 'We'll do something about it,' Charlie said, before Jack could answer.

'Like what?' Slink snarled. He looked at Jack again, and his voice was loaded with venom as he said, 'You can thank your lucky stars that I haven't seen my mum since we broke into the Facility.' He balled his fists. 'If she gets this, I-I just –'

'I know,' Jack said, raising his hands. 'I'd never forgive myself. We all care about her, Slink. She's part of our family too.'

'Family look out for one another,' Slink growled.

Jack winced and rubbed his chest. 'The only thing we can do right this second is stay away from everyone and try to find some kind of cure.'

Slink thrust a finger at him. 'I blame you for this,' he said through gritted teeth. 'You've killed us.' He turned around and limped away.

'Where are you going?' Wren called.

Slink didn't answer.

Wren went to go after him, but Charlie held her back.

'Let him calm down,' she said.

Wren ignored her and hurried away. 'Slink, wait up.'

Jack and Charlie watched them go.

'He'll come round once he's cooled off,' Charlie said, glancing at Jack. 'He knows it wasn't your fault. He's just angry, that's all.'

'He's right though,' Jack said in a quiet voice. 'I've killed us all.'

Charlie spun to face him. 'Stop feeling sorry for yourself and start thinking, would ya?'

Jack frowned at her. 'What?'

'*Think*, Jack. It's what you do best, isn't it? How do we put this right? How do we find a cure?'

Jack started pacing, hoping against hope that the movement would get his brain going and help him figure out what their next move should be.

If there was an antidote, then it wouldn't be just a case of popping into the local hospital and asking for it. The Medusa virus was a top-secret weapon, so the most logical place for an antidote to be located was...

He stopped dead.

Back at the Facility. The same place the virus was created and stored.

The workers at the Facility must have had access to the antidote there, just in case the virus was accidentally unleashed on them.

That meant the Outlaws needed to break into the Facility again and take it.

Wren returned with Slink a few minutes later.

Slink crossed his arms and didn't make eye contact with Jack.

'We need to go back to the Facility,' Jack said to them. 'They must have an antidote there, because –'

'That's where they stored the virus,' Charlie said, catching on.

'Exactly,' Jack said. 'But we have to see Noble first. We need equipment and gadgets if we're gonna break into the Facility again.'

He strode down the path and the others followed.

'What about the virus?' Wren said. 'Noble might catch it.'

'Why would Jack care about infecting someone else we care about?' Slink snapped. 'Don't matter, does it, Jack? Noble's old anyway. Who cares, right?'

'*Slink,*' Charlie hissed.

Jack tried his best to ignore the snide comments, but they cut deep. 'Noble's front door has a camera and an intercom,' he said in a monotone. 'We'll explain what's happened and come up with a way to grab a few essentials without coming into contact with him.' He glanced at Slink. 'That all right for you?'

Slink huffed and looked away.

'We're gonna need somewhere to stay too,' Charlie said, pulling her jacket collar up and coughing.

Jack's stomach sank as he remembered the last time he'd seen the bunker. 'Yeah,' he muttered, 'we'll think of something.' He shivered and wished he had his hoodie.

Charlie looked at him. 'We also need to make a quick stop before Noble's.'

Ten minutes later, they were standing in a car park behind a supermarket.

Slink kept an eye out while Jack and Charlie waited by a yellow clothes bank.

'I don't feel right doing this,' Jack whispered to her.

'It's an emergency,' she said. 'We'll donate back ten times what we take, and we'll take only what we need.'

Jack nodded.

The metal grille on the front of the clothes bank lowered and Wren peered out. 'Found something for Jack.' She pushed a bundle of fabric through the opening and Charlie took it.

Charlie shook it out and handed it to him – a purple hoodie with a fluffy collar.

'She has to be kidding,' Jack said.

'It's all there is,' Wren's muffled voice retorted from inside. 'Unless you want a nice blue evening dress?'

'Nah, you're all right.'

'Find something made out of thin material,' Charlie reminded her.

'I am, I am. Give me a minute.'

As Wren rummaged about inside the clothes bank, Jack slipped on the hoodie and felt instant relief from the cold.

Charlie smirked at the bright red bullseye logo on the front. 'Looks good.'

'Whatever.'

Wren's head reappeared and she handed Charlie a couple of shirts. 'Anything else?'

Charlie turned to Slink. 'Do you need anything?'

He shook his head and looked away.

Jack took Wren's hands and pulled her back out.

Once she was safely on the ground, wearing a dark pink cardigan with flowers, Jack looked over at Charlie.

She was tearing the shirts into wide strips.

'What are you doing?' he said.

Charlie handed him one. 'Tie it around your nose and mouth, like a bandana. It'll help us to stop spreading the virus.'

'Good idea.' Jack did as she said and pulled up his hood.

Once Slink and Wren had done the same, they hurried back across the car park in the direction of the Docklands.

It took Jack, Charlie, Slink and Wren a lot longer than it normally would to get across London as they deliberately kept out of the way of people, using alleyways and side roads.

Finally, they turned the corner into the road where Noble's warehouse stood.

They froze, and stared in disbelief.

'This. Isn't. Happening,' Charlie breathed.

The entire warehouse was ablaze. Flames burst from the windows and thick smoke billowed into the sky, blotting out the stars and moon.

'Oh my God.' Wren's eyes were full of tears. 'Noble.'

'He'll...' Jack swallowed. 'He'll be OK,' he said, although his trembling hands told him he feared otherwise.

Several fire engines were dousing the flames, but it was no use – the roof crashed into the building, releasing more smoke and fire into the night sky.

'This is karma,' Jack muttered.

Charlie glanced at him. 'What? Since when have you believed in anything like that?'

'It's because we set fire to the theatre.'

'That wasn't our fault,' Charlie said in a firm tone. 'That was an accident, Jack. This is Hect–' Her words choked off as she obviously came to the same conclusion Jack had reached – this was all Hector's doing.

Jack thought of Noble's collection – his antiques and priceless cars, all destroyed.

It was then that Jack noticed a black SUV parked further down the road.

'Move.' He grabbed Charlie and Wren's arms and pulled them back into the shadows. 'Slink?'

Slink followed, hands in his pockets, walking with a defiant look. 'What are you doing now?'

Jack coughed and pointed at the car.

'You think that's Hector's people?' Wren asked.

As she said it, a lower-floor window shattered and flames erupted into the night. Jack caught a glimpse of the SUV's driver. It was Connor, Hector's lead henchman.

The fact that he was still there and watching the building meant that he expected Noble to return. And that also suggested Noble wasn't inside when they set fire to it.

Jack let that thought ease his worrying slightly. 'We've got to get out of here,' he said.

'What about Noble?' Slink asked.

Jack looked back at the burning warehouse and prayed that he was right and that Noble wasn't in there. 'He'll be OK,' he said again. But he wished he could be one hundred per cent sure.

Jack glanced back at the SUV and had an over-powering urge to run over there and punch Connor in the face. But the moment wasn't right for any stupid actions – they'd lost the bunker and Obi, and now Noble and his warehouse too.

With a massive effort, Jack turned his back on the fire and marched between the buildings.

'What's the plan now?' Charlie asked as she, Slink and Wren hurried after him.

Jack stopped at the end of the alleyway and turned back to them. 'Slink and Wren, can you guys please go scope out the Facility?'

'And do what exactly?' Slink said with a heavy measure of sarcasm. 'We can't break in again because we don't have Noble's gadgets. We don't even have phones.'

'We've got to at least try,' Jack said. 'Look at what's going on. See if there are any visible signs they've increased security since our break-in. We need that antidote.'

'Fine,' Slink grumbled. 'Come on, Wren, let's go.'

'Wait.' She looked at Jack. 'What are you doing? How will we find you again?'

'We're going to find Noble, right?' Charlie said to Jack.

'Yeah.' Jack pinched the bridge of his nose. 'We need to make sure he's OK.'

'Not to mention the fact that Noble is our best hope of getting any help now,' Charlie added.

Jack lowered his hand and nodded. 'Only problem is, how do we find him?'

'The London Eye,' Charlie said. 'That's where Noble always meets us when we do joint missions. If there's trouble, I bet he goes there in the hope that we'll turn up.'

'You're right,' Jack said. 'Of course.' He shook his head, trying to clear the grogginess. 'If you need us, we'll be on South Bank,' he said to Wren.

Jack turned away and strode down the road with Charlie.

An hour later, Jack and Charlie were standing at the bottom of the steps of County Hall, right next to the London Eye.

Tourists took pictures and queued for the ride, oblivious to the danger a few metres away from them in the form of two very sick kids.

Jack had an overwhelming urge to scream at them to stay away or to run in the opposite direction, but the Outlaws needed Noble's help and causing a scene would be the worst thing to do.

Soon the London Eye would be closing for the evening, so at least there weren't as many people around as in the daytime. Even so, Jack gestured for Charlie to pull back, keeping as much distance as they could from the tourists.

'I don't see Noble,' Charlie said, standing on tiptoes to peer over the crowds. 'What if we infect him too?'

'We won't,' Jack said. 'We keep our distance, understood?'

She nodded and both of them made sure their bandanas were securely in position.

'Oh, thank God.' Charlie pointed. 'There he is.'

Noble had spotted them too and was making his way over to them. He was wearing a baseball cap and a long coat.

A huge wave of relief swept through Jack – Noble really was OK. But did he know about the warehouse? Did he know it was all Jack's –

'It's not your fault,' Charlie said, noticing Jack's expression. 'Hector burnt Noble's place down, not us.'

'It's payback for what we did to Hector's dad,' Jack said. 'If we hadn't got involved with the Del Sarto family in the first place, none of this would've happened.'

'No,' Charlie said, 'it would've been worse. You know that, Jack.'

Noble walked over to them, his concerned eyes taking in their bandanas and Jack's purple hoodie.

Jack held up a hand. 'Stay back. Not too close.'

'Are you all OK?' Noble asked, looking between the pair of them.

'Your warehouse...' Charlie said.

Noble sighed. 'I know.' He glanced about for a moment, his eyes scanning the crowds, then he looked back at them. 'Tell me what's happening.'

'We have a virus,' Jack said in a low voice. 'Hector infected us.'

Noble hesitated, then said, 'The Facility?'

Jack nodded.

'OK,' Noble said slowly, his face showing the deepest concern.

'Medusa is a virus, and we caught it,' Jack said.

Noble glanced over his shoulder, then turned back and let out a long sigh. 'I'm sorry I didn't see it coming.'

'None of us did,' Charlie said, before Jack could comment.

Noble seemed to be deep in thought. 'Something doesn't add up here.'

'What do you mean?' Jack said.

Noble looked at them both and kept his voice low. 'Ordinarily, I'd tell you to turn yourself in to the authorities, that they stand the best chance of containing the virus and stopping the contagion.'

'But it's too late,' Jack said, understanding what Noble was getting at. 'We've already spread it about London.'

'Yeah,' Charlie said. 'It was right after the Facility mission – way before we knew this was a deadly virus. We thought it was just a cold, and we went and got medicine and supplies. We started spreading the virus days ago.'

Jack and Charlie pulled back and turned their faces as a group of tourists scurried past them with their guide.

Jack's heart sank as he thought of the fire again and he looked at Noble. 'Your warehouse. I'm so sorry.'

'I know what you're about to say,' Noble said. 'It's not your fault. It's mine. I should never have shown Hector the warehouse. My mistake. We all thought he was a good guy.'

Jack was about to say something more, but Noble cut him off. 'I've been trying to call all of you. You don't have your phones, do you?'

'No.'

'I thought not. In that case, I just need to tell you that Obi is fine.'

Charlie gasped. 'Oh, thank God. You've heard from him?'

'Yes. He sent me a message through the Cerberus forum. Somehow Obi's kept his phone without Hector knowing about it.'

'Where is he?' Jack asked.

'He doesn't know. He said that Monday has him.'

'What else?'

'All Obi said was that they're keeping him in a locked office. He was blindfolded, so he has no idea where they took him, but he's pretty sure he's still in London. He says he knows Hector and his father aren't there because he's heard Connor talking to Hector on the phone.' Noble looked around then refocused on them. 'How did they get Obi? And why don't you have your phones?'

Charlie glanced uneasily at Jack.

Jack took a deep breath, opened his mouth and hesitated. 'We...' He sighed. 'I'm sorry, Noble. I lost the bunker.'

Noble's face dropped. 'No. You're joking?'

'I wish I was.'

'It's been raided,' Charlie said. 'Armed men. We didn't stand a chance. Happened too quickly.'

Noble looked at them in shock. 'Hector again?'

'Yes.'

'And what's your next move?'

Jack cleared his throat. 'We think the antidote is at the Facility. Somehow we're gonna break in again.'

Noble nodded. 'A lot of lives, including your own, depend upon it.' He pursed his lips and held out his phone. 'Take it.'

'No,' Jack said. 'We can't do that. *You* need it. We'll have to find –' He stopped. 'What the – ?' Jack stared, incredulous, as Slink and Wren hurried over to them.

'Noble,' Wren cried, obviously relieved he was OK. She rushed forward to hug him, but stopped herself and readjusted her bandana instead.

Noble smiled. 'Hi.' He looked at Slink. 'Are you all right?'

Slink shrugged.

'What's going on?' Charlie said. 'We thought you guys were going to the Facility?'

'We've been,' Wren said.

Charlie's eyebrows rose. 'That quick?'

'It wasn't there,' Slink said, crossing his arms. He looked at Jack. 'You remember that grey building?'

Jack nodded. The grey building housed the first security office that led to the underground Facility.

'Well,' Slink continued, letting out a breath, 'it's rubble now.'

'It's what?' Charlie said.

'It's been bulldozed,' Wren said. 'There's nothing left. The whole oil refinery is closed too. There's even a padlock on the front gate.'

Jack stared at them both. 'This just keeps getting worse.'

'Looky, looky,' a loud voice chimed.

Jack spun around.

Skin – a scrawny kid with a bald head, Talya's right-hand man – grabbed hold of Wren and pressed a knife into her side. 'Don't nobody move,' he warned. 'We wouldn't want this little one to get hurt.'

Slink went to lunge for him, but Jack grabbed his shoulder and pulled him back.

'Very wise of you, Jacky.' Skin grinned and looked at them all. 'Everyone, be calm.'

Behind him stood six other members of Talya's army, all glaring at Jack.

'Lovely night for it.' Skin looked at each of the Outlaws in turn, then at Noble. 'Who are you, Grandad?'

Noble stared back at him and remained tight-lipped.

'Too old to talk? Your tongue shrivelled up with age?' Skin looked at Jack, still grinning like an idiot.

'What are you doing here?' Charlie asked.

Skin gestured at the crowds of tourists. 'These are rich pickings. And you're on our turf 'ere.'

One of the other kids smirked, held up several wallets and a purse then slipped them back into his pockets.

Skin looked at Jack. 'Persephone's been asking after you, Jacky.'

'Who?' Slink said.

'It's Talya's nickname,' Jack replied, not taking his eyes off Skin.

'That's right,' Skin said. 'She really wants to 'ave a chat with ya. She's all eager about it. Won't shut up. "Find Jacky," she says. "*Find 'im. Now.*" We've had scouts on the lookout for ya night and day. We'd just about given up when...' He smiled and spread his arms. 'Lo and behold, look who should walk straight into our path.'

Skin's cronies chuckled.

'So,' he continued, slapping his hands together, 'we're all gonna go visit Persephone. Nice and quiet, like. No sudden moves. Got it?'

Jack looked at Noble. 'We'll see you later.'

'Oh, no, no, no, Jacky,' Skin said. 'Grandad's coming with us. Any friend of yours is a friend of ours.'

'No way,' Charlie said, stepping in front of Noble.

Skin pressed the knife harder into Wren's side and she winced. 'I insist, darlin'.'

Noble rested a hand on Charlie's shoulder. 'It's OK.'

She flinched from him, worried about infection.

Skin scowled at them. 'Move. Now.'

The four Outlaws and Noble, with Skin and Wren in the lead and Talya's six army members behind them, walked from the London Eye into a whole lot more trouble.

Talya operated out of a dilapidated warehouse in an old industrial estate not far from Battersea Power Station.

Skin and his fellow gang members marched the Outlaws and Noble in through the front door. It took a few seconds for Jack's eyes to adjust to the gloomy interior.

To their right was a desk. On it were several shoeboxes filled with items Talya's army had stolen from around London – wallets, mobile phones, jewellery – all picked from victims' pockets.

In the far left corner of the warehouse was a projector screen, with sofas in front of it, playing a comic-book movie. Explosions erupted, lighting up the walls in flashes of yellow and orange.

Much of the main floor was taken up by tents of various sizes and colours, with washing lines strung between them. Dominating the back of the warehouse were two double-decker buses parked next to each other. A bridge connected the upper decks and a lift was fixed to one side.

'This way,' Skin growled, and they followed him up the stairs of one of the buses.

On the top deck, Jack, Charlie, Slink and Wren sat squashed together on a sofa, while Skin shoved Noble into an armchair.

'You touch him again,' Slink snarled, 'and I'll make sure you never –'

'Ah, look what we have here.' Talya, a punky girl with spiky multicoloured hair and a crooked nose, wheeled herself across the bridge from the other bus. 'Wacky Jacky and his band of merry misfits.' Her wheelchair had gold-plated rims that glinted in the light.

Skin laughed. 'Good one, Persephone.'

'It must be Christmas already...' Talya spread her arms wide. 'Noble.'

Noble gave her a curt nod. 'Talya.'

'You know Grandad?' Skin asked her.

'Yes, I know him.' Talya looked at Noble again. 'I'm quite hurt,' she said, leaning back in her wheelchair.

45

'I ain't seen ya since...' she glanced at Jack, '*that* mission.'

'You mean the one where Scarlett died,' Charlie said.

'Yeah, that one.' Talya smirked. 'Well, you gotta expect some losses, don't ya?'

Jack's blood ran cold. The truth was, nothing would ever make up for the fact that Talya had sent Scarlett on a mission so dangerous it had killed her – and he hated Talya for that.

Scarlett had been the only one to come close to becoming the sixth member of the Urban Outlaws. Her skills were legendary – she was one of the best hackers Jack had ever known. She had understood instinctively how technology worked, she was an amazing actress and she was absolutely fearless. In fact, Scarlett was like all five Outlaws rolled into one and there could never be anyone else like her. Jack missed her so much, and it was because of Talya that he'd never see her again.

'Now then,' Talya said, eyeing them. 'What's with the bandanas? I wanna see your pretty faces.' She winked at Charlie. 'Especially you, princess.'

When none of them moved, Skin took a step towards them.

'We have the flu,' Jack said, and sniffed.

Talya frowned and wheeled her chair back from them.

Skin hesitated, then he took a large step backwards. 'Serious?'

'Yeah,' Jack said. '*Deadly.*'

They sat in silence for a long while, just staring at one another.

Jack finally opened his mouth to say something, but Talya cut him off.

'To save your silver tongue the trouble of trying to talk yourself out of this mess, Jack, I'm gonna ask you a question.' She held up an index finger. 'One tiny, teeny, simple question. If you answer it honestly – like, real honest – and I believe you, then you and your...' her eyes roamed over Charlie, Slink and Wren, '...little mates here might just live another day.'

Jack took a deep breath and waited.

Talya leant forward in her wheelchair and fixed him with a cold gaze. 'Did you deliberately do something to that cashpoint?'

Jack had been expecting the question, and for Talya to catch up with him sooner or later, but the timing was terrible.

He stared back at her and considered lying, but Jack knew she'd see right through it.

'Yes,' he said.

'What's she on about?' Charlie asked. 'What cashpoint?'

'You mean to say you haven't told your little mates here, Jacky?' Talya smiled. 'Yet you bang on, giving us the high-and-mighty act about how you're all so close.' She made quotation marks with her hands as she said, 'We're family.'

Skin laughed and waved a finger. 'Naughty, naughty, Jacky. You don't keep secrets from family, do ya?'

Charlie turned to face Jack. 'What is she on about?'

Jack hesitated. He'd planned on telling the others at some point – it was just that the opportunity hadn't come up yet.

'Spill it,' Talya said to Jack. 'Tell them what you did.'

Jack stared at the floor and sniffed. 'In exchange for a favour, I used a piece of software to hack a cashpoint machine.' He looked up at Charlie and braced himself.

Charlie frowned for a second, then her mouth fell open. 'Please tell me you didn't use that tool I made?'

Jack winced. 'Yeah. I did.'

Slink crossed his arms. 'I don't get it. What exactly did he do this time?'

Jack shuffled in his seat. 'I planted a special code so that any of Talya's army members could take as much cash as they wanted.' He looked between them all then his eyes rested on Charlie. 'It was the only way to get that confession from your dad's killer,' he said in barely a whisper.

Charlie scowled at him. 'Jack, I know you think you were doing the right thing, but –'

Jack held up a hand, cutting her off. 'That's not all.' He took a deep breath and continued, 'I also embedded another program in the cashpoint. I planted an extra code that called the cops any time one of Talya's gang tried to use it.'

Wren chuckled. 'I knew you wouldn't let her get away with it.'

Talya leant forward, her eyes intense, balling her fists. 'That is very unfortunate for you, Jack,' she said through gritted teeth. She paused a moment then looked at Skin. 'Kill 'em,' she snarled. 'All of them. Noble too.'

Skin pulled the knife from his belt and stepped towards them, the other gang members doing the same.

CHAPTER THREE

TALYA'S CRONIES GATHERED AROUND JACK,
Charlie, Slink, Wren and Noble.

'Get up,' Skin snarled, waving his knife.

Jack looked at Talya. 'You're making a huge mistake.'

'Oh yeah? How so?'

'Because I can offer you something a lot bigger, and you might want a piece of the action.'

Talya hesitated a second, then gestured at Skin.

He took a step back, looking extremely disappointed.

Talya nodded at Jack. 'Go on.'

'I can offer you something. Bigger than any cashpoint hack.'

'Why should I trust anything that comes out of your mouth?' Talya said.

'Morals,' Noble said.

Skin held up his knife. 'What you on about, Grandad?'

'Please,' Noble said, waving him off. 'Your threats don't bother me.'

Skin stepped towards him, knife flashing. 'They should,' he said, his jaw clenched.

'Enough,' Talya snapped.

With obvious reluctance, Skin stepped back again and tucked his knife into his belt.

Talya looked at Noble. 'Quit the riddles, old man. What are you goin' on about?'

Noble took a deep breath before speaking. 'You just asked why you should trust Jack ever again. And I said, "Morals."' Noble's eyes intensified. 'If you took the time to understand Jack's actions, you would realise when he's forced to lie, and why he has to do it. You can then turn that knowledge to your advantage. He lied to you about the cashpoint in the name of justice and what is right. This situation is different. He has no reason to lie now.'

Jack rolled his eyes. 'Thanks, Noble.'

'Being exposed as an honourable person is better than being stabbed, surely?' Noble replied.

Talya's eyes narrowed and her expression hardened further. 'All right then,' she said, looking directly at Jack. 'Let's see if I can grasp what goes on in that nutty head of yours.' She sat back, rested her elbows on the arms of her chair and interlaced her fingers. 'First of all, what d'ya mean, "in the name of justice"? Why did ya plant the extra code in the cashpoint so my army gets caught?'

Jack thought carefully for a moment before giving his answer. 'I just think stealing from innocent people is, you know...wrong.'

Talya balled her fists, seeming to fight back her rage. 'Wrong?'

'I couldn't live with myself if –'

'We weren't stealing from innocent people,' Talya shouted, her anger boiling over. 'The bank covers those losses, Jack. We were stealing from *the bank*, you complete –' She bit her knuckle and looked up at the ceiling.

A few seconds passed as Talya took slow breaths. She seemed to be trying to compose herself before refocusing on Jack.

'You're a fine one to talk,' she said. 'You steal from people all the time. You break into places and everything. We're not so different, now, are we?'

'We only take from bad people,' Wren said.

Talya's eyebrows rose at that. 'Bad, good – it's just perspective, little girl. You're not the cops or nothin'.' She waved a finger at them. 'It's not for you lot to decide who's good and bad, who should be stolen from or not. We do what we 'ave to.' She gestured at Skin and the six kids stood behind him. 'Just like you do to look after your family.'

'We don't keep all the money,' Slink said. 'We give most of it away.'

Talya laughed. 'How very decent of you. *Most*. You've done some right dodgy stuff in your time, the lot of ya. So don't go lecturing me with your holier-than-thou attitude.' She shook her head and looked at Jack. 'I think it's time you decided what side of the fence you're on.' Her eyes roamed over Charlie, Slink and Wren before coming to rest on Jack with an intensity he'd never seen in her before. 'You need to make up your mind whether you're a bad guy or a good one. No more playing both sides.' She waggled a finger at him. 'That's why you keep getting into all this trouble.'

Jack stared at Talya as her words sank in – in a twisted way, she was right. And he hated that fact.

Being an Urban Outlaw did mean they had to do some bad things to make sure good then prevailed, but Jack always knew their intentions were right. *Weren't they?*

But, for now, they had a job to do.

Talya considered Jack a long while, before finally speaking again. 'Planting that program in the cash-point – I can't make up my mind whether it was very brave or very stupid of ya.'

'Probably a bit of both,' Slink said.

Jack couldn't help but snicker at that.

Talya ground her teeth. 'Now,' she said slowly, 'before we get down to the meat of what this big piece of action you can offer me is, I wanna know something else. You see, what puzzles me is what exactly you're up to.' She leant forward. 'I can see it in them eyes of yours, Jack. I'm not your biggest problem right now, am I?'

Jack shrugged and tried to sound casual. 'We have a situation to sort out. That's all.'

'What is it?'

'Trouble I've got us into.'

'Oh dear. Well, that's sad, ain't it?'

Skin laughed.

'Shut it,' Talya snarled. 'No offence, Jack, but you're always in trouble. And it would appear that you owe me again. Your debts just keep mounting up, don't they?'

'Yeah, I suppose they do.'

'Now, I'll ask you one more time. What's goin' on?'

Skin's hand twitched towards the knife in his belt.

Jack glanced at the others and sighed. 'Fine. I'll tell you.'

'*Jack*,' Charlie hissed.

Slink crossed his arms. 'That's it, mate, get us into more mess.'

Wren shook her head, which promptly set her off coughing.

Charlie rubbed her back.

'Go on, Jack,' Talya said. 'I'm dying to know.'

'We have nothing left,' Jack said. 'The bunker is gone.'

Talya's eyebrows lifted. 'What? Your secret hide-out? What happened?'

'It was raided.'

Slink sneezed. 'We've lost everything.'

'That. Is. Precious.' Talya looked between the four Outlaws and laughed.

'It's not funny,' Wren said, bringing her coughing under control and scowling at her.

Talya's expression hardened again. 'What did you just say?'

'None of us is thinking straight,' Jack said. 'This flu ...'

'That's your trouble?' Talya said. 'You lost your hide-out? No wonder you didn't want to tell me – you're nothing without your little computers and gadgets, are ya? So, who did it? Who raided your precious bunker?'

'Hector's men,' Jack said.

Talya's eyebrows knitted together. 'Am I supposed to know who that is?'

'Have you ever heard of the Del Sartos?' Jack said. 'Benito Del Sarto and his son?'

Talya shook her head. 'Should I 'ave?'

'They're rich,' Charlie said.

'Good for them.'

'No,' Jack said, 'it's good for *you*.'

Talya considered him. 'How d'ya figure that?'

'We did a mission a while back. Broke into their hotel suite and took a very valuable painting.'

'How valuable?'

'Millions,' Jack said, with a straight face.

Talya snorted. 'Sure.'

'Check the news if you don't believe me. We sent the painting back to the museum in Boston.'

Jack saw Talya hesitate and knew that she believed him. After all, it was the truth this time.

Undoubtedly she'd still check his story out, just in case he was lying. She wasn't stupid.

'Go on,' she said.

'Well, the painting wasn't the only valuable item in that suite. There's loads of stuff up there. Antiques, more paintings – several rooms filled with it all.'

Talya frowned. 'Do I look like an antiques dealer?'

Jack let out a breath and kept his eyes locked on hers. 'Let's go there now. I'll tell you where it is and how to get in. There's a lot of money sitting up there. More than your gang would ever get picking tourists' pockets.'

'A *lot* more,' Charlie said.

Talya stared, and Jack could see the mental cogs whirring.

She licked her lips. 'I do know one guy who might be able to shift this stuff for us.'

Jack nodded.

There was a long, tense silence as Talya considered the proposed deal.

Jack tried not to make eye contact with Talya or to show her the slightest sign of weakness. He gazed at Skin and the other gang members by the door and his stomach knotted.

Charlie went to stand up. 'Can we go?'

'Not so fast, princess,' Talya said.

Charlie sat down again with a huff.

Here it comes, Jack thought.

Talya looked straight at Jack, her expression unreadable. 'All right.'

Jack stared. 'Pardon?'

'I said, all right. I'll send my army over to check the place out.' She leant forward in her wheelchair. 'No second chances though, Jacky. If you've tricked me again, I'll –'

'No tricks,' Jack said. 'I promise the stuff is there.' He held out his hand and they shook. 'You won't be disappointed.'

'I'd better not be.' Talya nodded at Skin.

Skin thrust a notepad and pen at Jack and he scribbled down the location of the hotel and the details of how to break in. When he was done, Jack handed it to Talya then, together with Charlie, Slink, Wren and Noble, he stood to leave.

'Wait a minute.' Talya tapped the notepad. 'How do I know what you've written here is right? Could be a trap.'

'You have my word,' Jack said.

'Your word?' Talya looked unimpressed. 'No offence, Jack, but your word means nothing to me any more. Not after what you've done and all your little tricks.' She nodded at Skin.

Skin stepped forward and pressed a knife to Noble's stomach.

'Get that thing away from me,' Noble said.

'Keep resisting, Grandad,' Skin snarled in his ear, 'and I'll gut ya.'

'We'll keep Noble until I'm satisfied you haven't tricked me again,' Talya said to Jack. 'I know how much he means to you. Once we have all that loot safely in our mitts, we'll let him go.'

'I can't agree to that,' Jack said.

'You don't have a choice.' Talya pointed a finger at the steps. 'Get out of 'ere before I change my mind.'

'I told you I can't do that,' Jack repeated, defiant. 'Noble's coming with us.'

'Oh, Jack.' Talya gave a heavy sigh. 'Why do you always have to make things harder than they need to be?'

'You're not keeping him here,' Charlie said. 'The deal's off.'

'Sorry, princess,' Talya said, waving her gang members over. 'But Jack already shook on it.'

Two of the tallest goons grabbed Jack, while the others shoved Charlie, Slink and Wren towards the door.

'You can't do this,' Charlie shouted.

'I can,' Talya said. 'And I have.'

'Get off me,' Wren screamed as one kid manhand-led her down the stairs.

A tall kid dragged Jack to the door by the scruff of his neck.

Jack looked back at Noble. 'I'm sorry.'

'It's fine, dear boy. Everything will work out.'

But Jack felt terrible.

He wanted to fight. He wanted to kick and punch his way out of there, taking Noble with him. But he knew Talya would never let any of them out of that warehouse alive.

No, the only way to keep Noble safe now was to find something else to trade – because Jack knew that even when Talya had all of the antiques from the hotel suite, there was no chance she'd let Noble go free that easily.

Jack could see the anger and hatred in her eyes, and he felt the same towards her.

Talya had to pay for Scarlett.

Somehow, in some way, he'd get his revenge.

The gang members bustled Jack, Charlie, Slink and Wren outside and slammed the warehouse door shut.

'We can't leave him,' Slink said, wheeling round on Jack.

Jack raised his hands. 'I'll sort this mess out, I promise,' he said with what he hoped sounded like confidence, although he felt exactly the opposite inside.

Slink huffed. 'It's your fault we're in all this mess in the first place.'

Charlie rested a hand on his shoulder. 'Calm down. It's not helping.'

Slink shrugged her off and crossed his arms.

'I know you'll work something out, Jack,' Charlie said.

'You always have done,' Wren added.

Charlie pulled a phone from her pocket. 'Figured we'd need this.'

Jack's eyes widened. 'Where did you get that?'

'From one of those boxes by the door.' Charlie smiled. 'Pinched it on our way out.'

'You are brilliant,' Jack said.

As they walked away from Talya's warehouse, Charlie connected to the internet and checked the Cerberus forum.

'Well?' Jack asked her.

'No messages.'

Jack groaned. That meant no more news about Obi.

'He'll be fine,' Charlie said, noticing everyone's crestfallen expressions. She didn't sound convincing though. 'So,' she said to Jack, 'what now?'

'Now?' Jack said, picking up the pace. 'Now we have to start work on finding that antidote.'

'But the Facility is gone,' Slink said.

'Yeah,' Jack said. 'But I've had a thought.'

'What?' Wren asked.

'I'm betting the antidote was stolen way before we got to the Facility.'

'Hector,' Charlie said. 'Of course. He would've taken the antidote. That way he can use it on himself, his dad and his men.'

Jack glanced between them. 'Exactly. We find Hector, we get the antidote.'

A while later, Jack, Charlie, Slink and Wren were standing outside the main entrance to a block of flats. Raze lived on the eighth floor with his mum and dad.

'Are we going to tell him?' Wren asked.

Jack shrugged. 'I'm not sure.'

They'd seen Raze, Wilf and Domino after the Facility mission, which meant they were infected with the virus too.

Slink turned to Jack, anger in his eyes. 'Don't you think Raze has a right to know what we've done to him?'

Jack nodded. 'Yes. Absolutely. But I want us to find a cure first. I don't want anyone to panic.'

Slink shook his head. 'You're wrong. He needs to know.'

Charlie frowned. 'You think he'd tell people?'

Jack offered her a weak smile. 'Wouldn't you?'

'Probably,' Charlie said, turning back to the door. 'I'd go to a hospital. I'd beg people to help me.' She coughed. 'It wouldn't be any use though, would it? No doctor can cure this.'

'No. And London would go into meltdown,' Jack said. 'If word got out that there was a deadly virus, people would panic and try to leave.'

'Spreading it about even more,' Wren said.

'Let's just go,' Slink said. 'If we're not going to tell him the truth we should leave him alone.'

'We need a laptop,' Charlie said. 'Jack can't do his hacking on just this, can he?' She held up the mobile phone.

'I thought he was supposed to be some kind of genius,' Slink muttered.

Jack adjusted his makeshift bandana and opened the door. 'Come on.'

Up on the eighth floor, Slink rang the bell and they waited.

After a minute, Slink said, 'Well, he's not in. Let's go.' He turned to walk away, but the door opened.

Raze blinked in the light. His hair was jutting out at all angles, his eyes were bloodshot and puffy, his skin was an almost translucent white and he was wrapped in a thick duvet.

He sniffed. 'All right?' He sounded terrible.

'Hey, mate,' Jack said, feeling awful about what they'd done to him.

The virus had obviously affected Raze far worse than the Outlaws – so far.

Raze sneezed, making them jump. He then wiped his nose on the duvet. 'Sorry.'

Charlie winced. 'It's OK.'

'My cold turned into the flu. Anyway, what can I do for ya?'

Jack took a deep breath and glanced at the others. It was then that he changed his mind. 'Can we come in for a minute?' he said.

'Sure.' Raze stepped aside. 'Mum and Dad are at work.'

Jack cringed at that – they would also be infected. Then their colleagues and their families too... How far had the virus spread already?

Raze's flat was neat and clean, with magnolia walls, wooden floors and dark furniture.

Raze dropped on to the sofa in front of a large-screen TV.

Jack, Charlie and Wren sat in chairs opposite, while Slink stayed standing by the door.

'So,' Raze said, looking between them all after a heavy sniff. 'What's the deal?'

Jack cleared his throat – it felt like sandpaper. 'You remember that Facility mission you helped us with?'

'Sure.'

'We were after a secret weapon,' Jack said. 'We, er...' He swallowed hard. 'Well, we found it.'

Raze looked curious. 'You did? I thought you said there wasn't anything in that place.'

'It was a virus,' Jack said in a low voice. 'And we passed it on to you.' He glanced at Slink.

'No you didn't,' Raze said. 'This cold started a day or two before the mission. I was sneezing and stuff, remember?'

Jack looked back at Raze. 'Yeah, we remember your cold. We thought we'd caught it off you at first, but it turns out that we have a virus. And you do too.' Jack sighed. 'You might have started with a cold, but you definitely have it.'

Raze blinked at them and looked dubious. 'I do? Are you sure about that?'

'Yeah,' Charlie said.

'We got tricked,' Wren said.

'*I* got tricked,' Jack corrected. 'I was tricked into carrying a virus out of the Facility, and now we're all infected.'

'OK,' Raze said slowly, now frowning. 'Let's just say I do have this virus – though I still think it's a stinking cold or the flu – is there a cure for it then?'

'Yes,' Jack said, with complete conviction. 'And we're working hard to get hold of it.'

Raze nodded and stared into space.

'We're really, really sorry,' Jack said after a moment, hoping Raze believed him because it was exactly how he felt.

Raze pulled the duvet tightly around himself. 'I assume it's that Hector's fault – he's the one, right?'

Charlie nodded. 'Right.'

'So what do you want me to do?' Raze said. 'How can I help?' He coughed. 'I might not be much use, but I'll try.'

'We just need to borrow a laptop,' Jack said.

Raze gestured down the hall. 'My room's the second door. There's a grey laptop by my desk and a bag on the floor.'

'I'll get it.' Slink strode off.

Raze went into a full-on coughing fit, before finally managing to compose himself again. 'What do I do?' he asked Jack.

'There's nothing you can do. We're working on it.'

'No,' Raze said. 'I mean about my mum and dad, my sister. Wilf and Domino too.'

'Oh.' Jack let out a slow breath. 'I can't ask you not to tell them, but it would be better if you didn't. Not until we've got the cure.'

'I still don't think I have a virus,' Raze said slowly. 'But I'll keep my mouth shut.'

'Thanks.'

Raze nodded. 'I trust you, Jack. You know that, yeah? You've never let anyone down.'

Those words made Jack's stomach sink too.

Slink returned with a blue bag slung over his shoulder. 'Thanks, mate.'

'No worries.'

Jack stood. 'We have to go. We'll update you as soon as we can.'

Raze sniffed. 'Punch Hector in the mouth from me, all right?'

Jack couldn't help but smile. 'Sure.'

As they walked away from the block of flats, Jack felt his guilt like a physical burden, crushing him into the ground.

Charlie noticed his expression. 'What now?'

Jack watched Slink and Wren walking ahead of them and kept his voice low. 'I don't think Raze believed us about the virus.'

'Does that matter?'

Jack shrugged. 'I don't know. Guess it's better that he doesn't. For him, anyway. I just hope we can sort all this mess out before, you know...'

'We can,' Charlie said, squeezing his arm. 'We will.'

Jack, Charlie, Slink and Wren sat on a bench over-looking the River Thames.

Slink handed Raze's laptop to Jack.

'Thanks.'

'I'm guessing you want me to tether it to the phone?' Charlie asked.

Jack nodded.

Tethering the laptop to the phone Charlie had taken from Talya would mean it had an internet connection.

After a minute, Charlie said, 'OK. Ready.'

Jack navigated to the Cerberus forum and was disappointed to see there were still no messages from Obi.

He then opened a command box and started typing.

'What are you doing?' Wren asked.

'Writing a tracer program so that you can follow whoever takes this laptop.'

'Wait a minute,' Slink said. 'We only just got it and now you're gonna let someone steal Raze's laptop? Are you crazy?'

'Not steal,' Jack said. 'I'm going to let them have it.'

Slink huffed in indignation, but Jack ignored him.

Once the tracer program was complete, he buried it deep within the laptop's software so no one would find it, then opened a new terminal box.

'Now what are you doing?' Charlie said.

'Hacking Cerberus.'

All three of them stiffened at this.

'You are crazy,' Slink said.

The Cerberus forum was one of the most secure and well-protected sites in the world. The rumour was that even the CIA and the British Secret Service had been unsuccessful in gaining access to it.

Jack continued typing lines of code.

'We know you're one of the best hackers in the world, but even you don't stand a chance of getting into Cerberus that quickly. No offence,' Charlie said. 'But wouldn't that take days?'

Jack glanced at them all and smiled.

'Oh no,' Charlie muttered. 'I've seen that look before.'

Jack hit the Enter key. He then installed a program on Talya's phone and handed it back to Charlie.

'Now that can trace the laptop,' Jack said, sitting back.

'Can you explain what you're getting us into now?' Slink said.

Jack stared out across the water for a moment. 'Not us. *Me*.' He looked back at them. 'We need the antidote, right?'

They all nodded.

'And in order to get the antidote, we need to find Hector. Right?'

They all nodded again.

'Hector uses the Cerberus forum to send messages to his people,' Jack continued. 'It's better than using phones, which can be traced. Cerberus is secure but it will still have a record of Hector's IP address on its servers somewhere.' Jack glanced at them. 'Cerberus is too well protected for me to hack into online.'

'Exactly,' Charlie said. 'Plus no one knows where the Cerberus servers are located. So how are you gonna do it, Jack?'

'Trent Myer,' Jack said. 'He's the guy that owns Cerberus. We get to him, I stand a chance at physically accessing the servers and finding Hector's IP address. I find that address, we work out where Hector's hiding, we get the antidote, we win.'

Slink shook his head. 'But you don't know where Trent lives either, do you?'

'No,' Jack said, looking out across the Thames again. 'You're right. I don't. But I have one way of finding out. I just have to get the Cerberus security guys' attention, which is what I've just done. They'll be on their way here right now.'

Everyone's eyes widened at that.

'They will?' Wren said, looking around.

Jack nodded. 'Cerberus have security specialists all over the country who can be anywhere at a moment's notice.'

'What do you want us to do?' Charlie asked.

'Hide,' Jack said. 'They're going to take me and the laptop to Trent Myer. I want you to follow the signal using the phone.'

'Then what?' Charlie said, getting to her feet.

'If I'm not out in an hour, work on a way to get me out.' He glanced at them. 'Go.'

All three of the Outlaws hesitated.

'Slink's right,' Charlie said. 'You've gone crazy.'

'*Go,*' Jack insisted.

With obvious reluctance, Charlie, Slink and Wren hurried away.

A minute later, a car screeched to the kerb behind him.

Jack sighed and pulled the bandana up over his nose and mouth. He heard footfalls and then a man wearing a black leather coat and gloves sat next to him.

'What are you doing?' the man asked.

Jack didn't bother to try to think of a clever answer. 'Looking for the IP address of one of your users.'

Several seconds passed before the man continued. 'Do you know who you're dealing with?'

'Yes. But I still need the IP address.'

'That's not going to happen.'

'Don't be so sure. Once Trent hears what I have to say, I'm betting he'll want to help.'

The man said nothing.

Jack looked at him. 'You've heard of Hector Del Sarto, haven't you?'

The man still didn't react.

'He and his father are spreading a virus, an epidemic that will destroy London. They have the antidote and we want it. No, wait – we *need* it. Everyone does.'

The man hesitated, then said, 'Who are you?'

'Achilles.' Jack saw the slightest recognition in the man's eyes. 'Feel free to check the video file in my Cerberus account,' he continued. 'Hector sent it. It will prove I'm telling the truth.'

There was a long pause then the man breathed, 'We'll look into it.' He took the laptop from Jack and slid it into the bag. 'Don't do anything else.' The man stood and started to walk away.

'Wait,' Jack said, getting to his feet. 'Aren't you taking me with you?'

'Not when you have a virus. Mr Myer wouldn't appreciate that.' He held up the bag with the laptop. 'I'll have to wipe this down too.'

The man turned and walked back to his car.

Jack watched him go and the other three Outlaws joined him.

'What went wrong?' Charlie asked.

'He guessed I already had the virus.'

'So,' Slink said, dropping on to the bench. 'Another dead end, huh?'

'Not entirely, no,' Jack said. 'They still took the laptop.'

'Which means we can trace it,' Charlie said, holding up the phone.

As the car drove off, Jack looked at her. 'Let's just hope it works.'

It could have played out better – he'd rather not have to break into Trent's house – but there was still hope.

The phone beeped and Charlie frowned at the display.

'What's wrong now?' Jack asked her.

'A message on the Cerberus forum for us.' Charlie gasped. 'It's from the Shepherd.'

'The Shepherd?' Jack said, incredulous. 'Tell him we haven't got time –'

'We're gonna have to make time,' Charlie interrupted, handing him the phone.

I KNOW YOU HAVE MEDUSA.
WANT THE ANTIDOTE?
MILLENNIUM BRIDGE.
NOW.

Twenty minutes later, Jack, Charlie, Slink and Wren were striding over Millennium Bridge. It was late at night and there was no one else around.

Halfway across they found the Shepherd, a red-haired man wearing a tailored suit. He was leaning against the railing and didn't look to be in a very good mood as they joined him.

'You know what?' he said in a slow, measured voice. 'A third of London's drinking water comes from this river.' He nodded over his shoulder at the Thames. 'Chances are, we've all drunk from it. Think of all the toxins, the human waste – not to mention it's also reckoned that one body a week is dragged ashore. Think about that for a second.'

'I'd rather not,' Jack said.

'They do clean the water, you know,' Slink said. 'We don't just drink it like that.'

'Even so.' The Shepherd turned his nose up and shuddered. 'Disgusting.' He looked between the

Outlaws. 'I wonder how many people you four would infect if you spat into that water.'

'How do you know about the virus?' Jack asked.

The Shepherd held up a USB drive. 'I believe this is yours.'

Jack winced. He'd accidentally left the USB drive in a computer in that house in Dryford Square. The Outlaws had broken into it to try and get information on the Facility's old director.

Another mission that ended in disaster.

'I know why you broke into the Repository,' the Shepherd said. 'I also know about the Facility. And the virus. What a horrendous mess you've caused.' He nodded to each end of the bridge as several men stepped on to it, wearing hazmat suits and breather masks.

'We didn't know it was a virus,' Charlie said, staring at them.

'It doesn't matter,' the Shepherd said in an almost bored voice. 'We have to contain you.'

'Look,' Jack said. 'We're trying to put this right. The Del Sarto family –'

'– have given us their instructions,' the Shepherd finished.

Jack blinked. 'What?'

'They're holding London to ransom.'

'How can they?' Charlie said.

'The military are moving in as we speak. They're isolating London, setting up emergency quarantine and shelters all around the M25. All planes are now grounded, all London airports shut down. We have orders to take you in – and that's exactly what we're doing.'

'Where's the antidote?' Charlie asked. 'You said you had it.'

'No, I didn't. I just asked if you wanted it,' the Shepherd said, as his men approached. 'Don't make this harder than it needs to be.'

'Please,' Jack said, desperate to make him see sense. 'We're trying to put this right.'

'You're too late.'

The men on either side drew nearer.

'Why?' Charlie said. 'Let us at least try.'

'No.'

Slink glanced left and right – the men were almost on them. *Go*,' he shouted.

The four Outlaws went to leap up and on to the bridge's railing but something hit Jack in the side of his neck.

He staggered backwards and was about to pull whatever it was off when there was a sharp pain and his entire body was instantly paralysed.

He watched helplessly as the others got hit too and their bodies went rigid.

Before Jack had time to think of a way to escape, the world spun around him and he lost consciousness.

CHAPTER FOUR

JACK AWOKE WITH A START AND SAT BOLT upright. He rubbed his eyes, blinked and looked around. He was in a narrow bed in a small room that reminded him of a prison cell – only instead of grey walls, this room had horrible, bright yellow walls and the floor was lime green.

In one corner stood a bookshelf with five dog-eared fantasy novels, several different Bibles and a dictionary. Opposite him was a giant mirror that filled the entire wall, and underneath that, bolted to the floor, were a table and two chairs.

There were also a couple of doors, one of which stood open and led to a bathroom. Jack's gaze moved to the door that was closed – it was made of polished metal and had a rubber seal running around the outside edge. It also had an electronic lock and its LED shone a solid red.

Jack stared at it and suddenly understood what this room was for: it was some form of quarantine. The Outlaws had been isolated from the rest of the world.

He swung his aching legs out of bed, cricked his stiff neck and glanced up. There was a security camera in the top corner above the door, watching him.

Jack heard footsteps coming from the hallway.

He stood, wobbling for a second then regaining his balance, and watched as the lock on the door clicked and the red light went out.

The door opened and the Shepherd walked in.

'What have you done to us?' Jack croaked. 'Where's Charlie? What did you do with Slink and Wren?'

'They're all perfectly safe.' The Shepherd gestured to one of the chairs at the table. 'Please sit down. We need to talk.'

Jack crossed his arms.

The Shepherd stared at him a moment. 'If you wish to find out what's happening to you, I suggest you sit.'

Jack thought about defying him further, but the truth was that he wanted answers – he wanted to know why the Shepherd had captured them and what his plan was.

With reluctance, Jack sat.

The Shepherd sat down opposite. 'I'm sorry about the poor accommodation and for knocking you out, but it was for your own safety.'

'Really?' Jack said, coughing. '*Our* safety? Right.'

'It is,' the Shepherd said in a flat tone. 'We couldn't allow you to know where we were taking you and your friends.'

'Don't you know it's wrong to kidnap people?'

'We didn't kidnap you,' the Shepherd said, without a hint of remorse or emotion. 'This is –'

'Quarantine,' Jack interrupted. 'Yeah, I'd kind of guessed that.' His brow furrowed as he thought of something he'd wanted to ask the Shepherd on Millennium Bridge, but hadn't been given the chance. 'If you know that we're infected with a virus, then why are you here? Why aren't you wearing a mask or something?'

The Shepherd levelled his gaze. 'I've taken the antidote.'

Jack stared back at him. 'What?' He felt a sudden surge of hope. 'You have the antidote? Where is it? Have you given it to us yet?'

The Shepherd held up a hand. 'Let me explain. The Medusa virus was developed ten years ago, along with an antidote.' He straightened his tie and continued, 'A normal virus can survive for around twenty-four hours outside a living host body. The Medusa virus is very special – it can lie in a dormant state on any surface for years, decades even. That's why it was never used – it was too hard to contain.' He sighed. 'Or kill.'

'Then why didn't you destroy it?' Jack leant forward and balled his fists. 'Why did you keep it alive at the Facility?'

'Fear,' the Shepherd said. 'It's a deterrent for our enemies. We leaked information about Medusa a long time ago.' A hint of a smile played on his lips. 'Our enemies are less willing to attack us if they think we'll unleash a genetically modified virus on them.'

Jack nodded. That made sense.

'The Medusa virus was never meant to be unleashed,' the Shepherd went on. 'It was considered far too dangerous. Even so, when Medusa was first created, I – along with the royal family, the prime minister and a few hundred top officials – took the antidote.'

'So,' Jack said, 'when do you give the antidote to us?'

The Shepherd shook his head. 'I don't.'

'What? What do you mean?' Jack said, aghast. 'Give us the antidote! What are you waiting for?'

'We don't have it. Your friend Hector stole it.'

A wave of dizziness washed over Jack and he wanted to throw up. His worst fear had been realised. Hector had the antidote, but now Jack, Charlie, Slink and Wren were trapped inside quarantine with no way to get to him.

The Shepherd glanced at the mirror then back again. 'When Hector's people raided the Facility, just before you got there, they stole the antidote along with records of its formula. They deleted all traces of it and left.'

'What about the scientists who made Medusa in the first place?' Jack said, desperation clawing at his chest. 'They must remember how they created it?'

The Shepherd shook his head again. 'Hector took care of them all.'

Jack swallowed and winced with the pain. He knew exactly what 'took care of them' meant. He shook his head. 'Hector used us to break in and unleash the virus on London.' He buried his face in his hands.

No matter what Jack did, whatever decisions he made, Hector kept on winning.

Now, millions of people could die.

After a minute, Jack lowered his hands. 'So what happens now?' he said in a hoarse voice.

'We have people trying to work on a new antidote, but it could take months, perhaps years, to get it right.'

Jack blinked. 'My friends might not even have a week left.'

The Shepherd nodded. 'A lot of people are going to die.' He said this without emotion, and Jack stared at him.

How can he be so cold?

'Wait a minute. Hector has the antidote and the proof is that he must have used it on himself and his dad, right? Because there's no way he's going to risk exposure without protection.'

The Shepherd leant back. 'Yes.'

'So,' Jack said, not understanding the problem, 'send in a team of SAS or whatever and take it from him. Break into wherever he is, get the antidote, then cook up a new batch and cure everyone.'

'We can't.'

Jack frowned at him. 'Why not?'

'Because we don't know where the Del Sartos are hiding.'

Jack didn't know whether to laugh or not. 'Come on. They must be somewhere in London.'

'We don't know that they are.'

'They must be,' Jack said, incredulous. He opened his mouth to say something about the Cerberus forum and how he was looking for an IP address so he could track Hector down himself, but something in the Shepherd's eyes made him hold back.

The Shepherd was staring at the mirror and didn't even look at Jack as he spoke. 'It doesn't matter anyway. Even if we did know where Hector is, we couldn't do anything.'

Jack couldn't believe what he was hearing. 'Are you kidding me?' His voice rose. 'People are going to die – of course it matters.'

The Shepherd interlaced his fingers, rested them on the table and spoke in his usual calm voice. 'Hector has been in contact. And he's assured us that if we try to find him, or if anyone working for him is arrested, the antidote will be destroyed.'

Jack snorted. 'And you believe him?'

'Hector and his father have taken the antidote already. They're protected. They have nothing left to lose.'

'Yes they do,' Jack said, defiant. 'The antidote is the only thing they have to bargain with.'

'I'm afraid,' the Shepherd continued, 'that without knowing exactly where they're hiding the antidote, we can't take the risk.'

Jack could not believe what he was hearing. 'So you're letting Hector hold you to ransom?'

The Shepherd didn't seem to appreciate this question. His eyes hardened. 'For the time being. But he'll slip up sooner or later. He's just a child.'

'You should know better than to let that fool you,' Jack said, making sure the Shepherd didn't forget their last encounter and the missions involving a diamond and a laptop. 'Besides,' Jack continued, 'Hector's dad has woken up – there's double the trouble now. They'll be working together.' He stared at the door for a moment and imagined tearing it down with his bare hands and bursting outside. Instead, Jack took a calming breath and looked back at the Shepherd. 'What do Hector and his dad want?'

The Shepherd levelled his gaze. 'First of all, they want the whole of London evacuated. Also, I have to send him proof that we have you in custody.'

'Let me guess,' Jack said, balling his fists as a new surge of anger tore through him. 'Hector wants you to kill us.'

'No,' the Shepherd replied in a level tone. 'He's happy with you dying from the virus's effects.'

Jack rolled his eyes. 'Nice.' After a moment, he glanced around. 'Why here though? Why do Hector and his dad want us locked up here in particular?'

The Shepherd inclined his head. 'This is the most secure facility in the world. No amount of resourcefulness and trickery will get you out. Hector is obviously wary of your skills and wants you locked up tight.' He glanced at the mirror yet again. 'I think you're lucky to be locked up in here – we're about to announce a state of emergency.'

Jack's eyebrows rose at that. 'You're not seriously going to evacuate London?'

'Hector and his father have given us twenty-four hours.'

Jack couldn't believe this was really happening. It had to be a joke. There were millions of people living in London – it would be pandemonium.

The Shepherd stood. 'I thought you had the right to know the facts at least. I've given you all the information I can. My hands are tied now.'

'Yeah,' Jack muttered. 'Thanks for nothing.'

The Shepherd glanced from the camera to the mirror then to Jack, and he spoke in a quick, hushed tone. 'Our resources are stretched thin trying to put plans into operation. We don't have time to find Hector even if we could. The Del Sartos will be watching out for us and if we make any false moves, they'll destroy the antidote. I don't know what their ultimate plan is, but I'd like to find out.'

'If someone got you the antidote, how long would it take you to copy it and make more?' Jack asked.

'We have the best scientists coming from all over the world,' the Shepherd said. 'I'm no expert, but if they had the exact formula, I'd say a day, a few days at most.'

Jack nodded.

The Shepherd straightened up, strode to the door, hesitated and turned back. 'Oh, and here you are.' He tossed Jack's USB drive to him.

Jack caught it and looked down at it. If it wasn't for his stupid mistake of leaving the USB drive at the archives, he, Charlie, Slink and Wren wouldn't be in this mess. They'd be free to try to stop Hector and his father.

When Jack looked up again, the door was closed and the Shepherd was gone.

Jack groaned, walked over to the bed and lay down.

They'd been caught.

Game over.

Jack's body ached. He felt so exhausted that all he wanted to do was lie there and sleep. Instead, he stared at the ceiling and thought of Noble. Would Talya let him go when she had all the Del Sartos' antiques in her hands? Jack doubted it.

He thumped the bed with clenched fists. *Talya.* He hated her almost as much as Hector. If they'd never met, then Scarlett...

Out of everything that had happened in Jack's life, the thing he most wished he could change was him not stopping Scarlett going on that stupid mission.

Jack closed his eyes and, despite not wanting to, he couldn't help himself. His thoughts drifted back to that day...

Jack sat next to Charlie at a bench in her workshop and watched as she screwed the battery case back together on a remote-controlled speedboat.

'All the electronics have to be watertight,' she said, rechecking each screw in turn and then running her finger around the rubber seal. 'The slightest bit of moisture gets in and we're done for. Not to mention having to make sure it doesn't short itself out when we fire up the EMP.'

The EMP was an Electromagnetic Pulse – a way to deliver a short burst of high energy, knocking out their target's electronics. Jack looked at the front of the boat and the dome that housed the EMP generator. With Charlie's help, they'd steer the remote-controlled speedboat up to a real, full-sized boat, hit the EMP and temporarily knock out their electronics, which would leave the boat dead in the water. The Outlaws would then use Stingray, their miniature submarine, to board the boat and retrieve the suitcase they were after. Then they'd slip away again.

Well, that was the theory.

Jack admired all the modifications Charlie had made to the remote-controlled speedboat. It had a low profile, sleek and angled like a stealth bomber, with matt black paint to help camouflage it at night, and a wireless camera was mounted just behind the EMP dome. Charlie had soundproofed the motor and made alterations to the hull in order to keep the boat's wake to a minimum, and a small antenna stuck out of the top which sent the signals back to the modified control – a standard remote with several extra buttons and two screens mounted on either side. With all the extras, the remote control was now so heavy that Charlie had needed to add a strap that fixed in place over her shoulders just so she could hold it.

Jack shook his head at the complexity and ingenuity of it all, as Charlie sealed the top back on. 'You really are great at this stuff.'

She smiled. 'Thanks. I did have a couple of brilliant teachers though.' She glanced at Jack. 'You think Talya will go for this?'

'I hope so,' Jack said. 'It's better than her way – the brute force approach that's likely to get people hurt.'

The Outlaws owed Talya a favour and now, in turn, had got caught up in one of her crazy schemes. Jack had argued with Talya, saying that there were plenty of opportunities to carry out the mission over the next week and asking that she sit back and let the Outlaws take care of it, but Talya was anything except patient.

Now he had to go back and convince her that this way would work. If only she'd just –

Suddenly, the door to Charlie's workshop burst open and Slink came running in. He looked pale and out of breath.

Jack frowned. 'What's wrong?'

'Talya.'

Jack's stomach sank. 'What about her?'

'She's going ahead with that mission.'

'You're kidding,' Charlie said, slamming the screwdriver down. 'When?'

'*Now*. Her gang are on their way.'

Charlie shook her head. 'She's crazy.'

'I told Talya it was suicide,' Jack said. 'Why can't she just listen to me?'

'That's not all,' Slink said, looking uneasy. 'Scarlett's with them.'

'*What?*' Jack leapt to his feet.

Slink nodded. 'Wilf just called me. Said he saw her leaving.'

'Where are they going?' Jack asked urgently.

'I told Wilf to follow them,' Slink said. 'He reckons they're down by Waterloo Bridge.'

Jack turned to Charlie. 'I have to stop her. It's too dangerous.'

'It's miles away,' Slink said. 'You won't get there in time.'

Charlie stood and looked at Jack. 'Yes, we will.'

'Thank you,' he said, and they sprinted from the workshop.

It was dark as Jack and Charlie ran down an alley-way and slid to a halt in front of a rusty metal skip.

Charlie quickly undid the padlock, released the clasp and hinged the entire side of the skip upwards, revealing her prized possession inside its protective cocoon – a customised MV Agusta motorbike.

Ordinarily, climbing on the back of Charlie's bike was an absolute last resort, but she was right – it was their only chance at getting to Waterloo Bridge in time.

Jack grabbed two helmets as Charlie wheeled the bike from the skip, handed one to her and got on behind her.

'No point me asking you to take it easy, is there?' he said.

'Nope.'

The engine roared to life, and they were racing down the alleyway and across London.

It was at least ten minutes before the bike slowed and Jack felt brave enough to open his eyes.

He looked around.

They were driving under Waterloo Bridge.

'Where's Wilf?' he said into the intercom.

'Ahead,' Charlie replied.

Jack peered over her shoulder. Sure enough, he could see Wilf standing by the lifeboat station.

Charlie drew up alongside him.

Jack jumped from the bike and pulled off his helmet. 'Where are they?'

Wilf pointed and, with trepidation, Jack turned to look.

He saw the silhouettes of at least thirty kids standing on the bridge. Twenty or so had already climbed over the railing and were securing ropes and harnesses.

Charlie took off her own helmet and rested it on the fuel tank. 'Oh no,' she breathed.

Jack didn't need to ask her what she'd seen, for in the centre of the group of kids was Scarlett, her unmistakable, long, wavy hair dancing in the breeze.

'I've got to stop her,' Jack said.

'Too late.' Charlie pointed at a luxury pleasure boat as it glided under the bridge.

Its upper deck was filled with men in suits and women in elegant dresses, all holding glasses of champagne and chatting as a live band played. Towards the back of the boat, Jack could make out the Mayor of London. He was talking to a businessman wearing a turban.

Jack looked on, helpless.

As soon as the boat emerged from under the bridge, the kids dropped down, landing on the roof of the pleasure boat and catching the guests by surprise. In an instant, they were shouting and storming the boat, brandishing clubs and knives.

Jack jogged along the bank of the river, watching as Scarlett and two other kids raced to the front of the boat and burst into the wheelhouse. One kid grabbed the captain, while the other took the wheel.

Scarlett turned to a cupboard on the wall and started picking the lock.

Charlie caught up to Jack. 'Talya's getting Scarlett to do it?'

'Yeah,' Jack said, balling his fists. 'She's the quickest.'

Meanwhile, the rest of Talya's gang were screaming and shouting, distracting the guests from what was happening at the bow.

Scarlett opened the cupboard and pulled out a briefcase. She turned to the kid at the wheel and nodded.

He yanked the wheel hard over, aiming for the shore.

With his heart threatening to burst through his chest, Jack increased his pace, with Charlie running alongside him.

When the boat was a couple of metres from the bank, kids started jumping.

Scarlett left the wheelhouse, with the other two following.

One kid on the bank gestured for the briefcase and she threw it to him. The kid snatched it out of the air and ran off into the night.

As the boat continued towards the bank, the other two kids with Scarlett jumped.

It was at that precise moment that she spotted Jack and her face dropped.

Jack stared back at her, unsure what to do or say.

Scarlett hesitated for a moment longer then, refocusing on the riverbank, she hunched down, ready to jump.

Jack suddenly detected movement in the corner of his eye – the captain was grabbing the wheel and throwing it hard over to avoid a collision with the shore.

As if in slow motion, Jack looked back at Scarlett.

As the boat swung from the riverbank, she leapt. Scarlett didn't stand a chance – the gap was now too great – and she hit the wall and toppled backwards, landing in the water with a heavy splash.

Jack watched, frozen in horror, as the back end of the boat fishtailed towards the bank, its motors churning the water where Scarlett had just fallen.

'*No!*' he screamed.

The boat moved away and Jack couldn't see her anywhere.

'*Scarlett?*' he shouted.

Charlie grabbed his arm and pointed, and her voice broke. '*There.*'

A few metres out, a body bobbed to the surface, face down.

Without thinking, Jack climbed on to the wall and jumped.

The icy water hit him like a sledgehammer, knocking the air from his lungs. Jack clawed his way back to the surface, and as soon as his head broke into the open air he was swimming towards her.

Jack reached Scarlett, rolled her over, cupped a hand under her chin and, with his free hand, scrabbled back to the riverbank.

'Here,' Charlie said, racing down a set of steps.

Jack swam to her and together they lifted Scarlett's body from the river and up to the bank, where they laid her down. Frantically, Charlie checked for a pulse, then turned her ear to Scarlett's mouth.

'Jack, she's not breathing!'

Jack shook her. 'Scarlett? Can you hear me? Wake up!' he screamed.

Hurried footfalls made Jack turn around.

Wilf was running towards them with two men in RNLI uniforms, both of them carrying medical bags.

Jack and Charlie backed away as the men set to work performing CPR, blowing in Scarlett's mouth and pumping her chest.

'Thanks,' Jack said to Wilf.

Wilf gave a curt nod and stared down at Scarlett.

Charlie grabbed Jack's arm as they watched, numb.

The last time Jack had seen Scarlett, she'd laughed at one of Obi's terrible stories. He could still see the dimples in her cheeks and the glint of mischief in her eyes.

But this story didn't have a happy ending.

Because Scarlett never did wake up.

CHAPTER FIVE

JACK WASN'T SURE HOW LONG HE'D BEEN lying on the bed staring at the ceiling, but he guessed a few hours had passed at least.

His body ached and a small part of him was glad of the short rest.

The virus was taking a stronger hold of him and he wondered how long it would be before he didn't have the energy to move any more. *Days? Hours?*

He was so tired but couldn't sleep – his mind was ablaze, an unfocused blur of thoughts and images.

A guy wearing a full hazmat suit brought him dinner: half a roast chicken with chips and a side salad, a two-litre bottle of water and chocolate sponge for dessert.

At first, Jack was going to refuse to eat it, out of protest. Besides, his throat was sore anyway. But he needed to keep his strength up.

Jack was taking several long gulps of water when the lock on the door clicked. He looked over at it – the red light had gone out.

He waited for whoever it was to enter the room, but no one came in.

A full minute passed and the light still remained off with the door unlocked.

Frowning, Jack stood and quietly approached the door, his senses on high alert.

He listened, but couldn't hear any sounds coming from outside.

Something didn't feel right.

Jack glanced at the camera in the corner of the room and was surprised to see it was now pointing up at the ceiling.

He remained still for a moment.

What's going on?

After a few more seconds, Jack took a breath, turned the handle and opened the door.

Before him was a long hallway lined with other steel doors. Jack was about to step out, when the door opposite his opened. He quickly pulled his door to, leaving a gap of a few millimetres to peer through.

Charlie stuck her head out and looked left and right.

'Charlie.' Jack opened his door fully. 'Are you OK?'

She nodded. 'You?'

'Yeah, I'm fine.'

Charlie glanced up and down the hallway again. 'This is creepy,' she whispered, her voice sounding croaky.

Two other doors opened, and Slink and Wren emerged.

Wren ran over to Charlie and hugged her. 'This place is horrible.'

'I don't think much of it either,' Slink said, joining them. 'I mean, who paints walls yellow with green floors?'

'What's going on?' Wren said, looking up at the camera in the hallway – it too was pointed at the ceiling.

'I think the Shepherd's letting us out,' Jack said slowly. 'But I don't know why.'

Charlie sniffed and looked at Jack. 'What do we do?'

Jack hesitated a moment, thinking. He looked at the camera, at the black door at the far end of the hallway, then back to the others. 'If we stay, there's a chance they might find a cure for us.'

Slink laughed, which promptly turned into a raspy cough. He bent over, hacking for a moment, then straightened up. 'Since when were you happy sitting around and waiting for someone else to maybe fix things, Jack?'

Jack looked at Charlie and Wren.

They both nodded.

'We need to get out of here,' Charlie said, pulling her hood and bandana up.

Jack agreed. The fact that Slink's coughing hadn't drawn attention meant there was no one else around. The coast was clear. For now at least.

'Come on,' he said, cricking his neck and wishing the Shepherd had given them all something for their stiff muscles.

Together, they hurried to the black door at the end of the hallway and Jack opened it as quietly as he could.

Beyond was a flight of stairs.

'Awesome,' Charlie groaned. 'Isn't there a lift somewhere we could use?'

'I feel fine,' Slink said, although his pale face, bright red nose and puffy eyes told a different story.

They stepped through and were about to walk up the stairs when Jack spotted something on the bottom step.

He scooped it up and handed it to Charlie. It was the phone she'd taken from Talya's warehouse.

Charlie frowned at it, then set the phone back on the stair.

'What are you doing?' Wren said.

'I don't trust it.' Charlie looked at Jack. 'Whoever's helping us escape could've fixed it so they can track us once we're outside using that phone.' She glanced down at it. 'God only knows what they've done to it.'

Jack hated to admit it, but Charlie was right.

'Is the Shepherd doing this?' Slink asked.

'I think so,' Jack said. 'Who else would it be?' He looked up the stairs and sighed. 'Come on, let's go.'

Jack's muscles ached with every step they climbed, and halfway up he was gripping on to the handrail.

He could tell the others were suffering too. Wren's face and hands were deathly pale; Slink was leaning more and more on his good leg; and Charlie's rasping breaths echoed in the stairwell.

Finally, mercifully, they reached the top. They walked through another door and found themselves in a hallway identical to the one below except for a security guard sitting in a chair next to the exit at the far end. His head was bowed and he seemed to be watching a movie on his phone.

The Outlaws froze on the spot, staring at the man, but he didn't look up at them.

Was the guy so engrossed in his film that he hadn't heard the door open?

Jack doubted it.

He looked at the others, unsure how to proceed.

Wren sneezed loudly, making them all jump.

She clapped a hand over her mouth and turned to the others with a horrified expression.

Jack immediately looked back at the guard, but the guard's eyes were still fixed on the phone in his hands. Jack's gaze moved to the door on the guard's right and the glowing exit sign.

There was nothing else for it – they had to try. He took a deep breath and signalled for Charlie, Slink and Wren to follow him.

Jack crept up the hallway, ready to run if the guard looked at them.

But, even as they got nearer, the guard still didn't flinch. Now they were closer, Jack could see the man's chest rising and falling as he breathed.

He was definitely alive. And his eyes were open, so he was awake too.

A shiver ran down Jack's spine and he glanced at the other three Outlaws.

They looked as unnerved as he felt.

Wren stiffened as the guard suddenly moved, and they all stopped dead in their tracks, staring at him.

But, instead of looking up, the guard turned to his left, still watching his phone – and now facing away from the exit.

Now Jack knew the guard must have been paid off or ordered to look the other way.

The only question was, by who?

Jack gestured to the others and they reached the door. He opened it and ushered Charlie, Slink and Wren past, before backing through himself.

Once on the other side, he let out a breath. 'Well, that was weird.' He turned around.

They were standing in a small forecourt surrounded by a chain-link fence.

Charlie pointed. 'Look.'

To their right was the unmistakable outline of the Secret Service building.

'The Shepherd let us out?' Charlie said in a hoarse voice. 'Just like that? No catch?'

'There's always a catch. We just don't know what it is yet,' Jack said, fixing the makeshift bandana over his nose and mouth.

Slink and Wren did the same with their bandanas.

There was a loud buzzing sound and a gate opposite swung open.

Without any further hesitation, the four Outlaws hurried through it, down a short driveway and on to the street.

The road was jammed full of cars, all beeping their horns and jostling for position. Each car was crammed full of bags, suitcases and people.

'They're trying to get out of London,' Jack said.

Charlie gasped. 'Because of the virus? Is Hector doing this?'

'I'll explain everything in a bit,' Jack said. 'For now, we need to get somewhere safe.' He gestured to a side path that steered them away from the mayhem, and pulled his hood up. 'Let's get out of here.'

Slink led the way. 'Where are we going exactly?' he called over his shoulder. 'The cavern?'

The cavern was a meeting place and a short-term shelter for homeless kids. If any child in London needed an emergency place to stay, then the cavern was it. It had food, water, bedding, clothes – everything needed to tide them over for a while.

Raze, Wilf and Domino checked the cavern daily and if any new kids turned up, they'd help them find their family, accommodation or anything else they needed.

The Outlaws often checked on it too and restocked its supplies, but, what with everything that had been going on lately, they'd hadn't gone to the cavern for a couple of months.

'There aren't any computers or phones stored there,' Jack said. 'We have to get on to the Cerberus forum and check to see if there are any messages from Obi.'

'We need a phone again?' Wren said, looking exhausted. 'Really?'

'I've got somewhere we can go hide out for a while,' Charlie said, putting her arm around Wren. 'We can catch our breath there.'

Jack, Charlie, Slink and Wren dodged crowds of panic-stricken Londoners and eventually came to an industrial building. A peeling sign above it read, *Caine Motors*.

It was Charlie's dad's old workshop – a place Hector didn't know about. There was no chance his goons would show up here.

A low, wailing siren sounded in the distance.

'What's that?' Wren said.

'It's getting worse.' Jack couldn't believe it was all happening so quickly – the Shepherd hadn't been exaggerating. He motioned to the door. 'We'd better get inside before the real chaos starts.'

'How could it get worse?' Wren asked.

'Don't you get it?' Slink said. 'Someone's told them all that there's a deadly virus spreading around London, so people are starting to freak out.'

'Get inside,' Jack said, glancing around uneasily.

Charlie unlocked the door and flicked on the lights.

The workshop looked the same as when Jack had last seen it, minus the Ford Escort Charlie had modified for their Facility mission.

After Charlie had got them a glass of water each, they sat down in the small office.

On the desk was an antique computer with a large, old-fashioned CRT monitor.

'Does that thing work?' Jack asked.

'Yeah, kinda,' Charlie said. 'It's got an old modem-type connection, but I've kept paying the bills so it should be OK.'

Jack flicked on the computer, and once it had booted up he logged into the Cerberus forum. 'Oh, thank God for that.'

'What is it?' Slink said.

'Good news – a message from Obi. He says he's fine. Still doesn't know where he is though.'

'How's he managing to keep his phone hidden?' Charlie said.

'I have no idea.' Jack smiled as he read Obi's message, feeling relieved that he was OK. 'He says he'll be in touch whenever they leave him on his own for long enough.' Jack read on and then frowned for a second. 'I don't believe it.'

'What?' Slink said.

Jack looked up at them. 'Do you remember when he was going on about the coming apocalypse? All that end-of-the-world stuff?'

Obi had all sorts of conspiracy theories and often bored the other Outlaws with them.

'Yeah,' Charlie said. 'I remember that one. He reckoned zombies would attack...' She groaned.

Slink smiled. 'Well, in a way Obi was right, wasn't he?'

'We're not zombies though,' Wren said.

'Nah, not yet.' Slink grinned. 'But it's still early days, isn't it?'

'So, what's actually going on then?' Charlie asked Jack.

'Well, Obi's not far off with his doomsday prediction.' Jack nodded at the TV on top of the filing cabinet. 'Does that work? I bet it'll answer some of your questions.'

Charlie walked over to the TV and turned it on.

Sure enough, a large sign appeared across the bottom of the screen:

NEWSFLASH.

Charlie turned up the volume.

'. . . being told to evacuate,' a female reporter was saying.

Behind her, a display showed a helicopter's view over London. Streams of traffic were leaving the capital like millions of ants.

'All airports in and around Greater London have been closed,' the reporter continued. 'These include Gatwick, Heathrow, Stansted, London City, Luton and Southend. The police and the army are advising that everyone remains calm.'

The screen divided, showing checkpoints with vehicles and people queuing to get through. Barbed-wire fences and the army held back crowds, while hundreds of medics checked civilians and led them to huge tents set up along the roadside.

'We now join Sophie Knowles on the ground.'

The main screen of the news channel was filled with the image of a reporter wearing a surgical mask and gloves.

The camera view spun round, showing the crowds pushing against the makeshift fences, shouting and screaming, while soldiers, with their weapons raised, barked commands at one another.

The camera abruptly swung to the reporter as she stepped inside one of the tents. There were rows upon rows of beds with men, women and children lying on them, being examined by medical staff.

The camera zoomed in on one small girl sitting on her father's lap as a nurse used a torch to look inside her mouth and behind her ears.

'This is crazy,' Charlie breathed. 'This is all because of the virus?'

Jack didn't respond. He couldn't.

The virus was disrupting people's lives and causing widespread panic. How long would it be before people were really hurt or killed?

The girl and her father were given tickets with numbers on them, then they stood up and the nurse led them from the tent.

The reporter and cameraman followed.

'Once preliminary checks are done,' the reporter said, 'people are taken into quarantine.'

The girl and her father were escorted to a large field surrounded by tall, makeshift fences. Thousands of other people were already crammed in.

'After one hour has elapsed,' the reporter continued, 'the potential evacuees are rechecked. If there are no signs of the virus present, people are then free to leave the city.'

Suddenly, the screen filled with the image of 10 Downing Street. The famous black door opened and the prime minister stepped out. He straightened his tie, walked into the road and stood in front of a bank of microphones.

He cleared his throat and read from a sheet of paper. 'I will be taking no questions at this time. As you can appreciate, we need to act fast. We urge everyone to stay calm during this national emergency. If you or your loved ones show any signs of having the virus, you will be taken into quarantine. Rest assured that we have hundreds of the world's best biologists working on a viable antidote.' He took a breath. 'We ask those of you who clear quarantine to proceed from the city in an orderly manner. Any sign of aggression will be met by force.' The prime minister cleared his throat again. 'We are unsure about the exact details of how this outbreak occurred, but we do know that a group of local terrorists are responsible. They call themselves the Urban Outlaws.'

The Outlaws gasped as an image of each of their faces appeared on the screen, including Obi's. The photos looked like they were taken from CCTV recordings at the time the Outlaws went to North Brother Island in New York.

'Hector's cameras,' Charlie said. She looked at Jack. 'He planned this all along.'

Jack felt sick and he was pretty sure it wasn't the virus making him feel that way.

The prime minister continued, 'If you see any one of these individuals, you are to consider them extremely dangerous. Do not approach them, but phone the hotline number that's scrolling along the bottom of the screen. There is a reward of five hundred thousand pounds for any information that leads to their capture.'

'Five hundred grand?' Slink said, wide-eyed. 'For that kind of money I might turn us in myself.'

The prime minister went on, 'We are working with the World Health Organization and many other countries are lending their full support in this critical time – this includes both medical and military assistance.' He looked directly at the camera. 'I do urge everyone in London to come to the border and have a health check. We've also set up several camps outside the main quarantine zone if you have no place to go. The army will patrol London, escorting any remaining citizens who are unaware of the situation to the quarantine border.'

'That's enough.' Charlie flicked off the television and turned to Jack. 'I can't believe this is happening. It has to be a nightmare.'

'My mum,' Slink said. 'I need to use that.' He waved a finger at the computer. 'Gotta tell her we're OK and make sure she doesn't go out.'

Charlie got up and let him sit in front of the keyboard.

As Slink typed, Jack stood up and started pacing the room.

'What are you thinking?' Charlie asked.

'I'm thinking we've got a lot of work to do. First, we have to find Obi and get Noble back from Talya, because we need all the help we can get to go after Hector and the antidote.' Jack gestured at the computer. 'And, no offence, if I'm gonna figure out where Hector's hiding, that thing is just too slow.'

'But I thought we had to break into Trent Myer's computer to find Hector?' Charlie said.

'We do,' Jack said. 'But we have to find him first, and I need a decent computer to get the tracer working.'

'From the program that you put on Raze's laptop?' Wren asked.

'Exactly,' Jack said. 'I need to send a signal to activate it. And in order to do that, I also need a fast internet connection.'

Slink sneezed, wiped his nose then moved away from the computer. 'Mum's fine.' Despite looking exhausted, he smiled. 'She reckons this virus is a load of rubbish. Says she ain't got a rash behind her ears or nothin'. I told her to stay put until I say otherwise.'

Jack felt relieved she was OK and hadn't caught the virus. That was one less thing to worry about. He supposed it was because she spent quite a bit of time in her apartment and had minimal contact with other people.

'So,' Slink said, leaning against the filing cabinet. 'Can you lot explain what you're talking about?'

Jack turned to him. 'In order to activate my tracer program on Raze's laptop and get into Trent Myer's private network, I need a proper, fast internet connection. I'm going to have to do a serious hack to get past his security. Noble will know how to help us do that. Which means that right now our only hope is getting him away from Talya.'

Charlie frowned. 'How are we going to do that?'

'And what about Obi?' Wren asked.

Jack held up his hands. 'We're gonna sort out both at the same time – my plan will get Obi and Noble back.'

'But how?' Charlie asked.

'By offering Talya something she can't resist.'

'And what's that?' Slink said.

Jack looked at them all. 'Why do you think Hector wants to evacuate London?'

They stared back at him for a moment, then Wren said, 'I know.'

'So, why?' Slink said.

'With London empty, Hector's free to break into anywhere he likes and take anything he likes,' Wren said. 'He can steal the Crown Jewels if he wants to.' She looked at Jack. 'Right?'

Jack nodded. 'Exactly. And I bet he's got his sights set on something big. So, we offer Talya a slice of Hector's action in exchange for Noble.'

A smile swept across Slink's face. 'We're finally gonna get Talya back for what she did to Scarlett, aren't we?'

Jack smiled back at him. 'Yes. That's the plan. But first, Obi. We need to find out where he is.'

The others didn't make a sound as they watched Jack think through his plans.

In the end, he realised there really was only one way to do it. Only one course of action they could follow.

And that also meant they'd only get one shot at getting it right.

Finally, after running through the mission a few times in his head, Jack looked at the others. 'OK. Plan formulated.'

'Is it dangerous?' Slink asked.

'Of course.'

'Then I'm in.'

Jack turned to Charlie and Wren – they looked pale and drawn. 'If you –'

'We're fine,' Charlie interrupted, though none of them was anywhere near fine.

'We're not dead yet,' Wren said. 'And if we really are gonna die, we need to take Hector with us.'

Slink rubbed his hands together. 'Finally someone's talking some sense.'

'Have you got radios of any kind?' Jack asked Charlie.

She thought for a few seconds, then clicked her fingers. 'Dad's old bike intercom system.'

'Enough for all four of us?'

'Yeah. Why?'

'Can you get them working, please?'

Charlie nodded. 'Come and help me, Wren.'

The two of them left the office.

Jack sat back at the computer, typed lines of code for several minutes and grumbled under his breath about the mind-numbingly slow internet connection he had to work with.

After rechecking everything had worked as he'd expected, he stood up and Slink followed him into the main workshop.

Charlie was at a bench with a drawer full of batteries and several walkie-talkies in front of her. She plugged in an earpiece and pressed the mic button on one of them.

'What about this one, Wren?' she said. 'Can you hear me?'

Wren was at the other end of the workshop. 'Yep,' she replied.

Charlie looked at Jack. 'We've got four sets working.'

'Great,' he said, waving Wren over to them. 'We need to hurry.'

'What have you done?' Slink asked.

'I've made it look like we're back at the bunker,' Jack said. 'Now, listen carefully...'

An hour later, Jack sat hunched in the corner of the platform at Badbury Underground Platform, partly obscured by a pillar. It was pitch black down there and the abandoned station was eerily quiet. Normally there was the constant rumble of Tube trains. Without them, it was like the city had no blood pumping through its veins – without the Underground, London was a lifeless corpse.

Jack stayed still, staring into the darkness in the direction of a door that he knew was on the other side of the tracks.

He ducked his head inside his jacket and pressed the mic button on the radio intercom. 'Charlie?' he breathed.

She answered, 'Yeah?'

She was the only one in range that he could talk to.

'Are you sure they came down here?' Jack whispered.

'Positive,' Charlie said. 'I saw them.'

Jack sighed. He'd been sitting in this position for almost twenty minutes and the only movement he'd detected was a rat scurrying past his feet.

'Keep a lookout,' he said in a hushed tone. 'And tell the others to do the same. We can't afford to make any mistakes.'

'Understood.'

A noise made Jack's head snap up and a sliver of light appeared ahead of him.

The door creaked open and Jack could make out two figures stepping through.

'...was a waste of time.' The lead man had a phone pressed to his ear and Jack recognised his voice.

It was Hector's number-one henchman, Connor. He crossed the tracks.

'I understand that,' Connor said into the phone. 'But someone has obviously tricked you. There was no one there. Have you checked in with the Shepherd?' He stopped as he listened. 'Right. I understand that too,' Connor said through gritted teeth. He hung up and made a snarling sound. 'And I don't appreciate being spoken to like a moron by a jumped-up little kid.' He glanced around then strode along the platform.

Jack quietly got to his feet and breathed into his microphone, 'He's coming.'

Jack counted to five then slipped Charlie's torch from his pocket, cupped his hand over it and used the dim light to follow.

Charlie, Slink and Wren were positioned at strategic vantage points around the area – Slink was on the roof of a block of flats that was so high he could see for miles – so they could watch where Connor went after he left. Connor must have parked a car somewhere nearby.

Once the team had spotted him, Jack and Charlie would then follow at a safe distance on her motorbike. Most of the roads in the local area were already empty and, with a huge amount of luck, Connor would lead the Outlaws straight to where the Del Sartos were hiding Obi.

Jack ascended a short flight of concrete stairs, pushed open a hatch and stepped into a narrow alleyway. He hurried to the end of it and glanced left and right.

'Where is he?' Jack whispered into the headset.

Connor was nowhere to be seen.

'Guys?'

There was still no answer.

Jack pulled the walkie-talkie from his pocket.

The display was dead.

CHAPTER SIX

JACK STARED AT THE BLANK DISPLAY ON THE
walkie-talkie, trying to think of a quick solution.

He smacked the side of it.

It still wouldn't turn on.

No.

He flipped it over, slid off the battery compartment and turned the batteries around a few times for good measure.

Nothing.

Jack swore under his breath and looked about.

It was eerily quiet, and he had no way of telling which way Connor had gone.

He hesitated and was about to turn left when he heard hurried footfalls.

'Hey.' Charlie came jogging up to him, out of breath and wheezing. 'What's going on?'

Jack held up his walkie-talkie. 'It's dead.'

'Here.' Charlie swapped it with hers.

'Thanks.' Jack put in the earpiece and pressed the microphone button. 'Guys? Guys, did you see him?'

'No,' Wren replied.

'Me neither,' Slink said.

Jack groaned and shook his head.

Charlie leant against the wall as she fiddled with the walkie-talkie. 'What do we do?'

'Wait,' Wren said. 'Yes, I see him now. He's gone right.'

'Yeah, I've got him too,' Slink said. 'Go right, Jack, then head towards the bridge.'

'Charlie, this way,' said Jack. With utter relief, he did as they said and hurried to the end of the road.

Charlie held up the walkie-talkie. 'It's working again.'

'Good.'

'I'll get the bike.' Charlie turned and strode down a side street.

Jack stayed put. 'Guys?'

'I've lost him again,' Slink said.

'It's OK,' Wren said. 'I can still see him. He's just going under the bridge now.'

Jack kept close to the buildings and hurried in that direction.

When he reached the concrete bridge, he slowed his pace and squinted into the darkness.

He couldn't make out any sign of movement.

'Bet he's parked under that somewhere,' Wren said.

Jack stopped, unsure whether to follow or not.

'Anyone see the other side of the bridge?' he asked.

'Not from here,' Wren said.

'Me neither,' Slink said. 'This is stupid. I'll try and get into a better position.'

'No,' Jack said. 'Stay where you are.' He'd carefully picked the vantage points for them so they covered the widest area possible.

Jack took a breath. He had to go in there himself and see what was happening.

He kept close to the wall, staying in the shadows as much as possible, and crept towards the underpass. He reached the edge, peered around the corner and could just make out a black SUV parked at the far end.

'He's gonna come out on the east side,' Jack whispered into his headset. 'Get ready.'

He glanced back over his shoulder and saw Charlie's bike speeding towards him.

Jack looked forwards again, just as a set of rear lights glowed red and an engine roared to life.

Charlie stopped alongside him and handed Jack a helmet, and he leapt on to the back.

He plugged the walkie-talkie into the helmet's microphone and headset. 'Wait a minute, Charlie,' he said, as her fingers twitched on the throttle. 'We can't let him spot us.'

'I know,' Charlie said, sounding agitated and ready for the chase.

They watched the SUV pull from the tunnel and turn left.

'What are you waiting for?' Slink asked. 'Connor's getting away.'

Jack adjusted the chinstrap on his helmet. 'You can still see him though, yeah?'

Slink and Wren both replied with a resounding 'yes'.

'You know what to do,' Jack said. 'Guide us.'

Directed by Slink and Wren, Jack and Charlie kept several streets behind Connor's SUV, but after just a few minutes of them twisting and turning through London's streets, only Slink still had eyes on Connor.

Jack could feel Charlie tense more with each passing moment.

Before long, Slink's panicked voice filled their ears. 'I'm losing him, Jack. He's heading towards the business district and there are too many tall buildings blocking my view.'

'No choice then.' Charlie opened the throttle and wove left and second right, until they could see the SUV ahead of them.

Jack ground his teeth. Most of London was dark now, and it wouldn't take much for Connor to spot them in his rear-view mirror.

'Hang back,' Jack said, squeezing her arm.

She shrugged him off. 'No way, Jack.'

'Better to lose them for now than get caught,' Jack said.

The SUV turned left.

Charlie stopped at the end of the road.

Before Jack could protest, Charlie turned the bike around, opened the throttle and shot back the way they'd come.

'What are you doing?' Jack said.

'I'm on it.'

They reached the Thames, but instead of following the road next to it, Charlie bumped on to the pavement and drove along the footpath. They were running parallel to the SUV – Jack could see it to their left every time there was a gap in the buildings.

He smiled and relaxed slightly – Charlie had it under control.

The SUV turned off the road and went behind a high-rise office block.

'We're losing them again,' Jack said.

'No, we're not.' Charlie twisted the throttle and accelerated along the path, then took a hard left and shot back on to the main road.

Ahead, the SUV had parked next to a set of bollards and Connor was striding towards a tall glass building.

Charlie turned off the bike's engine. 'They're hiding Obi in there?' She shook her head. 'Can you believe it, Jack?'

'Actually, I can,' he said.

It made perfect sense – the Millbarn building was the first place the Outlaws had laid eyes on Hector's father, Benito Del Sarto. Del Sarto Senior had been pretending to be an accountant by the name of Richard Hardy. That was also the first mission that had led them to all these problems.

Jack looked up at the tenth-floor, far-right-corner window, to where he knew Del Sarto's rented office was, though of course Hector and his dad wouldn't be stupid enough to hide out there.

In a way, now Jack thought about it, it made sense that the Del Sartos had demanded their men take Obi here – it was Hector sticking his fingers up at the Outlaws. Hector and his dad were probably laughing about how clever they were, picking a location to hide Obi where Jack thought they'd never return to.

Jack balled his fists.

Charlie turned to look at him. 'Is this gonna be a problem?'

He nodded.

The Millbarn building's security had individually key-coded doors, biometric scanners, many CCTV cameras and pressure sensors under the carpets, which was the reason Jack had chosen a different plan for that particular mission – they'd wound up using a modified telescope on a rooftop across the street.

He let out a breath. 'Let's go. I need some time to think.'

Back at Charlie's dad's garage, Jack brought Slink and Wren up to speed with what they'd seen.

By the time he'd finished, they both looked despondent.

'Well then,' Slink said, sitting on the desk and crossing his arms. 'That's the end of that then.'

'No, it isn't,' Jack said.

'We can get to Obi?' Wren asked.

'Of course we can.'

'Hold up,' Slink said, frowning. 'I remember you saying the Millbarn building had some of the best security you'd ever seen.'

'Exactly,' Charlie said. 'It took you months to plan a way around it.'

Jack nodded. 'I know.'

Now they were all frowning at him.

'So,' Slink said, 'is it impossible?'

'Not any more,' Jack said.

'What do you mean?'

Jack pulled up a chair and sat down with a heavy sigh. 'What's different from the last time we were there?'

'People,' Wren said. 'There's no people because of the evacuation.'

Jack smiled. 'Right. No people, which means no security guards and the police have their hands full already.'

'Ha.' Slink slapped his leg. 'So, no need for gadgets or nothin'. If the alarm sounds, who blinkin' cares? We can just bust a window and walk right in.'

'Yeah, something like that,' Jack said. 'But, if I can play it right, it won't be us who does the busting. It'll be Talya.'

A loud bang made them spin to face the door.

'What was that?' Wren whispered.

There was another loud bang.

'Someone's trying to break in,' Charlie hissed.

'Out,' Jack said. 'Now.'

The four of them hurried into the main workshop.

There was a third bang and the sound of splintering wood.

Jack, Charlie, Slink and Wren raced to the back door at the rear of the workshop.

It was padlocked shut.

Charlie fumbled with a set of keys as her hands shook uncontrollably. 'Blinkin' virus. It's winding me up.'

Jack spun back towards the front door as three men burst into the garage. *'Hide.'*

The Outlaws crouched down behind one of the cars that was covered in a dust sheet.

Charlie waved the key at Jack. 'Got it,' she mouthed.

Jack held up a hand and whispered, 'Wait.'

He peered around the corner.

One of the men was a police officer; the other two were dressed in army uniforms and had their weapons drawn. All three of them wore breather masks and latex gloves.

'I saw kids go in here,' the policeman hissed to the others. 'Lights are on. They must be hiding somewhere.'

The men split up and started searching the garage, looking under worktops and lifting dust sheets.

Jack waited for the coast to become clear and then signalled to Charlie.

Keeping low, she edged to the door, reached up, undid the padlock and quietly opened it.

With his heart in his throat, Jack held up a hand again as one of the men passed right in front of them. But he didn't look in their direction.

Jack waited until he was gone, then signalled.

Charlie ushered Slink and Wren through, then turned back.

The dust sheet on the car to Jack's left was suddenly yanked off, and one of the army men shone a torch through the windows.

'Don't move.'

Jack spun to his right, and to his horror the policeman was now standing on the other side of the car's bonnet, his feet planted shoulder width apart, gun aimed.

Jack leapt to his feet, ran to the door and shouldered Charlie, taking her with him.

They hit the ground outside and rolled.

A fraction of a second later, the two army men burst through, their weapons drawn.

'Hands above your heads,' one of them demanded.

'What do you reckon the chances are that they'll shoot us?' Charlie breathed to Jack as they scrambled to their feet.

Jack hesitated. It was a tough –

'Doesn't matter,' Charlie said. 'Decision made.' She turned on her heels and ran in the opposite direction.

Jack let out a small groan, then raced after her.

'Stop,' one of the men shouted.

Jack's shoulders hitched up as he braced himself for a gunshot. Mercifully, it didn't come, and he followed Charlie around a corner and along an alleyway behind the industrial units.

The ache in Jack's chest made him feel woozy. Every breath, every step made him wince.

To make matters worse, it started raining.

He glanced back to see both men were in pursuit.

'Why are we always running?' Jack shouted as he looked forward again and hurried past a skip and a stack of crates after Charlie.

She darted through a narrow gap between two buildings.

'If we didn't annoy people so much,' she said over her shoulder, 'we wouldn't have to.' She stopped at the end and looked about, breathing heavily and clutching her chest. 'You know what we haven't done for a while?'

Jack turned around and saw the two men running into the alleyway behind them. 'What?' he wheezed.

'Blind faith.' Charlie ran across the road at full pelt.

'No, Charlie, please.'

But it was too late. She vaulted the railing on the other side and disappeared.

The rain was torrential now.

Jack wiped water from his face and glanced back at the men. In a few seconds they'd be on him.

He turned back around and took a juddering, painful breath. Then, head low, he ran across the road and leapt over the railing.

On the other side was a steep embankment. Jack's feet slipped on the wet grass and, before he could get a grip, he was hurtling down it, out of control.

'Just relax,' he heard Slink saying. 'Let your body go limp.'

Easy for you to say, Jack replied in his head. Relaxing was a little difficult to do, especially knowing that at the bottom of the embankment was a –

Jack's legs slammed into something hard and he tumbled head over heels like a Catherine wheel. The world spun about him so fast he didn't know which way was up.

He braced himself and closed his eyes, resigned to his fate, and just hoped there was a hospital still open somewhere in London.

A second later, Jack cried out in pain as he slammed into a concrete wall and crumpled to the ground, winded and feeling like every bone in his body had been shattered.

Rain continued to soak through his clothes.

Charlie grabbed his arm and pulled him to his feet.

Jack gasped, shivering. 'Thanks.'

'Well, Jack,' Slink said, sauntering over to them with Wren in tow. 'I'll give you nine out of ten for the impressive acrobatics, but a two for the landing. What happened?' He grinned.

'I don't know.' Jack coughed and winced at the pain in his chest. 'Guess my thoughts were focused on trying not to die.'

Wet clothes, coupled with his aching muscles, the pain in his chest and his throbbing legs, made Jack wish he could curl up in a tight ball and sleep.

'You didn't relax, did you?' Slink pressed.

'Relax?' Jack wheezed, incredulous. 'How can I relax knowing we have a fatal virus, when London is being evacuated, Noble –'

'We'll talk about it later,' Charlie interrupted. 'Come on.'

As they hurried off, Jack looked up at the top of the embankment and saw that the two army officers were shadowing them from the path above.

Great.

Why couldn't they just leave them alone?

Jack, Charlie, Slink and Wren reached a bridge. Underneath was a steel door recessed into the wall.

Charlie opened it and they hurried through.

On the other side, she flicked on her torch then bolted the door from the inside.

They stood there for a few seconds and then heard footfalls running past.

When all was silent again, Charlie turned back.

Jack was hugging himself and his teeth were chattering.

She frowned at him. 'We need to go somewhere warm and dry.'

'Probably best, yeah.'

'That means there's only one place we can go,' Slink said. 'It's the last place we have left to hide.'

'The cavern?' Wren asked.

'The cavern,' he said.

Charlie handed her torch to Slink.

'Cheers.' Slink marched down a narrow concrete corridor, with Wren hard on his heels.

Charlie half-smiled at Jack. 'It's dry tunnels all the way there.'

Jack, his limbs aching, his chest hurting, followed them.

As they walked, Charlie talked to him, obviously trying to keep him alive or something.

'So,' she said, 'what's the plan once we eventually find out where Hector's hiding out?'

'Do what we always do,' Jack said through juddering breaths. 'Beat Hector, only to have him trick us again.'

Charlie glanced back at him and Jack caught her frown in the faint, reflected torchlight.

'Why don't we just make this the last time Hector sets us up?' she said.

Jack nodded. 'Deal.' The truth was, if this virus killed them before they could find Hector, he'd never need to trick them again.

Jack's body was telling him that time was rapidly running out, and all the hurrying around wasn't exactly helping matters.

They turned right, ducked through an archway and strode along a narrow path next to an underground river.

The concrete was green with algae and slippery underfoot. Jack stayed as close to the wall as possible and focused on his every step.

As another stab of pain shot through Jack's chest, he tried to remember how far the cavern was because he was becoming less and less sure he could make it.

Just when Jack was about to give up, they reached the underground entrance to the refuge.

The door itself was three metres high, over two wide, and made of heavy oak. Slink grabbed the cast-iron handle and swung it open.

Beyond was a vast cave with stalactites hanging from the ceiling, like the teeth of a demon, at least ten metres above their heads. The cavern's natural plateaux and crevices stored rations and cooking supplies.

In the middle of the cave was a pool of blue water and around it were several tents and beds.

'Wow, I've never seen this place so quiet,' Wren said.

Jack nodded. Usually the cavern was filled with kids.

To the right was a row of lockers. Charlie walked over to a locker, removed several towels and chucked one at Jack.

'Thanks,' he said, slipping off his hoodie and wrapping the towel around himself.

'You need to get out of those wet things.' Charlie took a pair of jeans from the locker, followed by a T-shirt and a coat. 'Wear these for now.'

Grateful, Jack did as he was told.

Wren handed him a pair of thick woollen socks. 'Here.'

Jack slipped them on and gave an audible sigh of relief.

Charlie then scooped up his wet clothes and strode over to a firepit near the pool.

She hung the clothes on a rack, as Slink knelt by the pit and lit a fire using a lighter and paper. Once it was going, he threw on a few logs and beckoned Jack over.

'Sit here and get warm with us, mate. We'll soon dry off.'

The flames grew, lighting up the cavern and sending shadows dancing around the walls.

Jack sat next to the fire and felt the heat penetrate his skin and work its way to his core.

He wondered how close to death he'd been – how much time he'd shaved off his life by getting so cold.

Slink sat next to him and rubbed his hands together. 'I feel horrible. I've never even had the flu before.'

'I'm really sorry,' Jack muttered.

Slink shrugged. 'It's all right.'

Jack sighed. Even if Slink did forgive him, it made little difference. Unless they could find Hector, they were all dead.

Jack looked at the tents by the pool. 'What do you think the chances are that someone left a laptop in any of those?'

'Slim to none,' Charlie said, joining them.

'I'll have a look anyway,' Wren said.

She walked over to the first tent, unzipped it and stuck her head inside.

A second later, Wren cried out and scrambled backwards, almost tripping over her own feet.

A head emerged from the tent and blinked at her. 'Wren?'

Jack couldn't believe his eyes. It was Wilf.

Wilf squinted at Jack. 'All right?'

'What are you doing here?' Charlie said.

Wilf yawned. 'Where else would we go?'

'*We?*' Jack said.

More faces appeared from a couple of the other tents around the pool.

'What's going on?' Domino said. 'I'm trying to sleep here!'

'Hey, guys,' Ryan said, climbing out of the tent next to Wilf's and stretching.

Ryan was tall for a ten-year-old, and had short, blond hair and blue eyes. His speciality was pretty much anything to do with sport or involving water. The Outlaws hadn't seen him since the O2 Arena mission when he wakeboarded up the Thames.

He waved at them all and smiled.

Wren backed away. 'Are you lot crazy? You'll get the virus.'

Jack got to his feet. 'Come on,' he said to the other Outlaws, 'let's go.'

'There's no need,' Domino said, climbing out of her tent and straightening up. 'We're not gonna get it.'

Wren circled them and joined Jack, Charlie and Slink.

'How do you figure that out?' Slink said.

'Because,' Wilf said, clambering out of his tent and joining the other two, 'you lot came to see us after the Facility mission, right?'

Jack nodded, thinking back to when they'd returned to the guard's flat, let the guy go and thanked the others for their hard work on the mission. 'We remember,' he said. 'So what?'

'So what?' Wilf folded down the flaps of his ears. 'No rash. See?'

'No rash?' Jack repeated, incredulous.

'The news said the first sign of the virus is a rash behind the ears,' Ryan said.

'We ain't got one,' Domino said. 'Never had one neither.'

Jack groaned and sat back down. 'If you haven't got the virus, it means you were lucky and didn't catch it off us the first time around.'

'Yeah,' Slink said. 'Have you seen Raze?'

'What about me?'

All eyes moved to the door as Raze walked in with a bag slung over his shoulder.

'What are you doin' here?' Slink said.

Raze smiled. 'I feel better.'

The Outlaws stared at him.

'Say that again,' Charlie said.

'I said I feel better. Not perfect, but definitely a lot better than I did.'

Jack shook his head. 'That's not possible.'

'Yeah, it is.' Raze dropped his backpack next to the fire. 'You see, I never got that virus. Like I told ya before – I had the flu or something.' He looked directly at Jack. 'Says on the news that the virus starts with a rash behind the ears. Well, you never asked me about no rash. Never had one, did I?'

Jack stared at him. 'You didn't?'

'Nope. Neither did my mum or dad. They got caught up in all that stupid panic and left London. I gave them the slip as we left. No way I'm leaving. Why would I? I figure it'll all blow over and everyone will come back.' He sighed. 'I'd offer for you guys to stay at my place, but the cops are all over it after they spotted me. Probably nicking my stuff.'

145

Jack winced. 'I lost your laptop. I'm sorry. I'll get you a new one.'

Raze shrugged. 'I know you're good for it.'

'Wait,' Charlie said. 'Back up a minute.' She looked at Raze. 'How's that possible? How have you not got the virus?'

'They ain't got it either,' Raze said, waving a finger at Domino, Wilf and Ryan.

Jack stared, trying to clear his head.

The Outlaws had had a rash behind their ears, which meant they definitely had the virus – there was no doubt about it. But why didn't the others? They'd been in contact just...

Jack gasped.

'What?' Charlie said.

'No way.'

'*What?*' she repeated.

'No. Flippin'. Way,' Jack shouted. He ground his teeth as he realised what was happening. Now it all made sense. 'That complete and utter...'

CHAPTER SEVEN

JACK PACED THE CAVERN, ANGER TEARING through him as he thought about what Hector had done.

More tricks.

More lies.

It has to stop.

Jack turned back and looked at Ryan. 'I gather you've watched the news recently?'

Ryan nodded. 'Bits. Kinda hard not to, y'know?'

'Did you ever see a report of more people being infected? Like, anyone at all?'

Ryan shook his head.

Jack spun around and roared.

'What's going on?' Ryan asked.

Jack faced the group again. 'Hector's tricked all of us. Again. That's what's going on.'

'We don't have the virus?' Wren asked.

'*We* do.' Jack pointed between the Outlaws. 'The four of us, and Obi.' He paused as anger and relief warred inside him. 'But,' he continued, 'no one else has it and no one else will get it. Hector has used us.' Jack dropped next to the fire and stared at the flames.

Hector had done it yet again.

After several seconds of silence, Ryan said, 'Are you lot hungry?'

Charlie gave him a nod, but kept her eyes on Jack.

Ryan strode off to the other side of the cavern and returned a minute later, his arms laden with sandwiches, crisps and biscuits. He handed them out, along with a bottle of water each to Jack, Charlie, Slink and Wren. Grateful, they drank.

Jack took small sips and winced with the pain – his throat felt raw. He looked at the sandwich in his lap and decided to give it a miss. He set it to one side and took another small sip of water.

Slink coughed. 'So,' he said to Jack, 'we've got the virus, but no one else has. Why? How's that possible exactly?'

'I don't know,' Jack said. 'But we can assume that we're not contagious.'

'How did we get it in the first place then?' Wren asked.

Jack shrugged. 'No idea. Maybe it was only contagious for a short while.'

'If this is true,' Ryan said, sitting down, 'why has everyone evacuated London?'

'Because they don't know that it's not contagious,' Jack said. 'Because Hector lied – he manipulated everyone else too. He did everything he and his father are best at.'

'Well, let's tell everyone then,' Raze said. 'We'll let them know they've been tricked.'

'Oh, yeah,' Slink said. 'Great plan, mate. I'm sure they'll believe us.'

Charlie nodded. 'He's right – they won't. Hector made sure that people think we're the enemy now.' She looked at Jack. 'We need proof Hector's lying.'

'So, now we need an antidote for us five, and, on top of that, proof that Hector's been lying to everyone.' Slink rolled his eyes. 'Well, *that* should be easy.'

'When is it ever easy?' Jack got to his feet, determined to put things right once and for all. This was their last chance, and he had to do it before the virus killed them.

'Where are you going?' Domino asked.

'We have a mission to finish.' Jack balled his fists. 'And it's time I go and see Talya.'

The other Outlaws moved to stand up, but Jack gestured for them to stay put. 'I need to do this one on my own.'

'No way,' Charlie said, getting to her feet. 'At least let me come.'

'No. Look, Charlie, I –'

'Shut up,' Charlie snapped. 'You always say we're a team. I'm coming with you whether you like it or not.' She put her hands on her hips. 'No arguments.'

'I'm coming too,' Wren said.

Slink stood. 'Me three.'

Jack held up his hands. 'No. Listen to me, guys – this is far from over and I need you two to stay here. Please? Trust me. It's only going to get harder from here on in and I need you to keep your strength if we're going to live through all of this.'

Slink hesitated then nodded. 'Fine. Whatever.' He sat down again. 'Just make sure you get Noble back, OK?'

'That's the first thing I intend to do.' Jack turned to the door, gritted his teeth and, as he and Charlie left the cavern, decided exactly what the next course of action needed to be.

He was going to make Hector, Del Sarto and Talya pay for everything they'd done. For all the people they'd hurt. But it would take every ounce of strength the Outlaws had left in them.

Jack and Charlie stood in the shadows a little way down the road from Talya's warehouse.

In the distance, they heard sirens and gunshots. It was like London had turned into a war zone.

Charlie gestured towards the warehouse. 'What's going on? What are they up to?'

They'd only been there a few minutes and already they'd seen around fifty kids coming and going, carrying various boxes and bags.

'That can't all be from Hector's hotel suite,' Charlie said. She glanced at Jack. 'Can it?'

'No,' Jack said. 'She's up to something. I'm just not entirely sure what it is.'

They watched for a couple of minutes more.

'So,' Charlie whispered to Jack, as two kids carried a wooden crate into the warehouse, 'what's the plan to get Noble out of there?'

Jack kept his focus on the building and his thoughts turned to Scarlett.

Talya was like Hector – she'd caused so much suffering and she didn't care who she hurt or how she got money. She didn't care that Scarlett had died, and Jack hated her for it.

Jack let the anger fuel him, bringing a surge of determination and renewed energy with it. And, for the first time in weeks, he could think clearly again.

He knew exactly what to do.

Charlie noticed his expression. 'Are you OK?'

'Never better,' Jack said. 'If I need you, I'll shout. I'm sorry, but I have to do this part by myself.'

He took a breath and strode towards the warehouse.

He was about to make another deal with the devil, but he was determined to win this time.

Jack marched straight through the warehouse door and once he was inside he recognised valuables from Hector's hotel suite. There were two giant vases, many oil paintings stacked against the wall, sculptures and several items of furniture.

On the desk by the door was a wooden box Jack had seen in the suite, containing three sets of diamond-encrusted cufflinks and a gold watch, all engraved with Del Sarto's initials.

By the looks of it, Talya had completely emptied the hotel suite and Jack was impressed that she'd managed to get everything back here.

But that wasn't all – kids were still coming and going with boxes and bags, slowly filling up the warehouse.

Skin appeared from behind a stack of crates and walked over to him. 'Well, looky, looky, it's wacky Jacky.'

Jack shoved past him.

'Wait a minute,' Skin said. 'You can't just barge in 'ere like that. You need an escort. Can't have you wandering about the place.'

Jack ignored him, strode up the steps to the top floor of the double-decker buses and was relieved to see that Noble looked unharmed. He was sitting in the same armchair and seemed relaxed.

'Hello, Jack.'

'Hi,' Jack said. 'How are you feeling?'

'Fine. No signs of the virus.'

There wouldn't be, Jack thought.

Skin ran up the steps and grabbed him. 'What the 'ell do you think you're doin'?'

'It's OK,' Talya said.

Skin let go.

Talya was sitting in front of a writing desk with a laptop open. 'I don't seem to be able to get any internet,' she said.

'You won't,' Jack said. 'In case you haven't noticed, London's been evacuated.'

'Oh, I've noticed, Jack,' Talya said, with an equal measure of sarcasm. 'That's why me and the gang are still 'ere, like.'

Jack turned to face her. 'Of course. There's no one around to stop you nicking stuff.'

Talya winked. 'We've now moved on to bigger and better things than your mate's hotel suite.' She waved a finger at him. 'I should thank you, really – you gave me the idea, didn't ya?' Talya grinned. 'While all the kitties are away, the mice will run and play.' She looked him up and down. 'How's the virus coming along? You're looking peaky. Shame you might die 'n' all.'

'You will too,' Jack lied. 'You'll get the virus sooner or later.'

'Not one single member of my crew has this so-called virus. I reckon it's a myth.' Talya shrugged. 'Anyway, Noble here tells me you're gonna track down the antidote, so even if I'm wrong, we're all saved, ain't we?'

'That's the plan.' Jack gestured to Noble. 'Come on. We're going.'

Noble stood.

'Not so fast,' Talya said.

'You have the antiques from Hector's hotel suite,' Jack said. 'A deal's a deal.'

'No deal,' Talya said. 'Why would I care about them antiques when the whole of London is up for grabs? What would I do with a few poxy trinkets?'

Jack let out a breath. 'What do you want now, then?' But he'd already predicted what the answer to that would be.

Noble sighed and sat down again.

'Well,' Talya said. 'Apart from the antidote, of course, I wanna know what's up with this Hector kid.' She pointed at one of the televisions. 'What's he doing all this for? Noble won't share. Took me hours to get him to tell me you're gonna be the hero and save London by getting the antidote.' She leant forward in her wheelchair. 'Tell me about Hector. What does he want?'

Jack shrugged. 'Who knows? Hector and his dad are lunatics.'

'Nah,' Talya said. 'I don't buy that for a second. You know what they're doing this for, don't ya? I just saw that look on your face.' Talya drummed her fingers on the arm of her chair as she seemed to think for a moment. 'Crown jewels? Bank of England?'

'Excuse me?'

'Please don't play dumb with me, Jack. You know exactly what I'm on about.'

Jack smiled inwardly. Talya was playing right into his hands.

'Look,' he said, making sure he kept a straight face. 'I can't just let you –'

'Let me?' Talya said, her voice rising. 'Who do you think you are exactly? *Let me?*' She ground her teeth for a moment and then seemed to compose herself. She waved a finger at him. 'You want Grandad back? Then you're gonna find out exactly what this Hector kid has targeted and what his plan is – because it's gotta be big.'

That was one thing Jack and Talya agreed on. With London empty, Hector would be stealing some-thing on a monumental scale – but what Hector had set his sights on, Jack had no idea.

Talya continued, 'And once he's inside wherever it is, my gang will move in.'

'Hector's men will have guns,' Jack said.

Talya waved that comment away. 'I have hundreds in my crew. We'll use all of 'em. Rush Hector and his goons. We might lose a couple on the way, but the rewards...' Talya licked her lips, obviously thinking of all the money she could make from the raid.

She leant forward in her chair and locked her gaze on his. 'What's your idea?'

Jack let out a slow breath. 'Hector will have everything mapped out. He's methodical. So if we go now, he'll have done the hard part already – he'll have planned whatever mission he has in mind and all we need to do is steal those plans and his equipment.'

'That's a stupid idea,' Talya said. 'We don't want his plans.'

'Yes,' Jack said in a firm tone. 'We really do.'

'No, we don't,' Talya retorted in an equally hard voice. 'We should wait until they've stolen the stuff and we'll take it from them. Let Hector's people do all the heavy lifting.'

Jack shook his head. 'You're wrong.'

'Excuse me?'

Skin took a step towards him. 'You want me to –'

Jack stifled a fake yawn. 'Enough with the threats.'

'It don't 'ave to be a threat,' Skin snarled.

Jack looked at Talya.

She signalled for Skin to step away and said, 'Go on then, Jacky. Stop messin' about and explain yourself.'

Jack cleared his throat – it felt like he'd swallowed hot coal. 'The hardest part of any mission is the planning. I should know. If you plan it right and have a good team, the rest is plain sailing, yeah? A bunch of trained monkeys can't muck it up if you have a good plan to start with.'

Jack waited for Talya's response and hoped she didn't see through him.

Luckily, Talya's ego did exactly what he'd hoped for and, after a moment's pause, she nodded.

'So,' Jack continued, reeling her in. 'When they do the job, Hector will use armed professionals, right? They'll be on high alert. They'll be ready for problems. Once they have the jewels or gold or whatever it is they're after, they'll protect it with their lives. But if we go right now…'

'They won't be expecting a hit,' Talya said, understanding him.

'Exactly.'

'And how do you expect to find Hector and his people?' Talya asked.

'We already know where they're hiding and we already know how to break in. We could just do with some extra help.'

Talya eyed him. 'Extra help? You need help from me, Jacky?'

'I don't *need* your help,' Jack said, trying to sound casual. 'It would just make life a bit easier. That way, we both get what we want quicker.'

He sat back and watched her mull that one over.

'So,' Talya said after several moments' quiet reflection, 'what've you got in mind? What's the mission?'

Jack fought to contain his smile.

An hour later, Jack, Charlie and Wren were standing across the road from the Millbarn building.

The whole area was eerily quiet – the streets were empty and there wasn't a single sound coming from anywhere.

Jack was relieved that Noble was now free from Talya, but the Outlaws' dealings with her were far from over. When Jack had explained his plan to Noble, he had thought that Noble was going to stop them. In the end though, when Jack asked Noble to play an important part in it, he had agreed.

Charlie leant into Jack's ear. 'Let me get this straight,' she said, frowning. 'You told Talya that Hector's hiding in there when he isn't?'

Jack nodded.

Charlie continued, 'And you told Talya that if she helps us break in, she'll catch Hector and his men with the amazing plans for a mission they're supposedly organising?'

Jack nodded again.

'All this so you could trick Talya into helping us break Obi out?'

'Yes.'

Charlie frowned. 'And you think this is going to work?'

Jack sighed. 'Not you as well. Noble said the same thing to start with.'

'Well,' Charlie said. 'You have to admit it, Jack – you're playing a dangerous game.' She glanced about. 'You actually think that Talya will come here? That she'll show up?'

'Yeah, she'll come.'

'And what happens when she finds out you've tricked her again – that Hector's not here at all?'

'I'm hoping we'll be far away when that happens,' Jack said. 'Besides, I've taken care of that too. Noble should be making a phone call as we speak.'

Charlie still didn't look convinced. 'What makes you think Talya will come here herself? She hardly ever leaves the warehouse.'

'I'm telling you – she'll come,' Jack said with utter conviction.

'But how do you know for sure?'

'Because I asked her not to.' Jack shrugged. 'After that cashpoint job, she doesn't trust me. Plus she has one major flaw.'

Charlie looked puzzled. 'What's that?'

'Talya doesn't trust her team either,' he said. 'Not with a prize as big as she thinks this one is.' He turned back to the building. 'She'll be here.' Jack coughed and rubbed his chest.

Wren sneezed and sat on the ground with her back against the wall.

'Are you OK?' Charlie asked her.

Wren shook her head. 'Not so much.'

'Me neither,' Charlie said, hugging herself.

Jack knew that the sooner they got Obi out of there and reunited the Urban Outlaws, the stronger they'd be to take on Hector.

Sure enough, a few minutes later, a London taxi with blacked-out windows pulled up to the kerb down the road.

Skin hopped out with six other kids, opened the back of the taxi and folded out a metal ramp. Talya wheeled herself down it and towards the Outlaws.

As she approached, she gave Jack one of her smug grins. 'All right?'

Jack glanced at Charlie as if to say, '*I told ya so.*' Then he looked at Talya again.

'Where's the rest of your gang?' Jack asked.

'Waitin' around the corner. I wanted to make sure this wasn't another one of your pathetic tricks.' Talya gestured to the Millbarn building. 'This it?'

'Yep.'

'Doesn't look so bad.'

'It won't be – with your help and once Slink disables their cameras,' Jack said.

'Is he inside?' Talya asked.

Jack shook his head and pointed.

Towards the top of the building was a figure, dressed all in black. Slink was climbing with no ropes or harness, and Jack's stomach clenched, remembering when Slink had fallen off the crane. His ankle still wasn't fully recovered. That, on top of having the virus, made this mission even more dangerous.

Talya smiled. 'He's got some guts, that one.' She glanced at Jack. 'When this is all over, I'm gonna take him from you. I could use his skills. Oh, and speakin' of skills ...' She looked at Charlie. 'All right, pretty girl?'

Charlie glared back at her.

Jack ground his teeth and focused on Slink as he scaled the last few metres and hauled himself on to the roof.

Charlie pressed the mic button on her walkie-talkie. 'Slink?'

'Here.'

Jack looked at the entrance of the building and then his eyes roamed over every floor. All was quiet.

'Go in as planned,' he said.

The sound of Slink removing an air vent cover came over the walkie-talkie's speaker. 'Give me a couple of minutes,' Slink said.

They all waited in anxious silence.

'Tell me exactly what's happenin,' Talya demanded, losing patience.

Jack took a deep breath. 'Slink is going to head down to the security office on the ground floor and turn off the external cameras but leave the internal ones on for now. Then –'

'Wait a second,' Talya interrupted. 'I thought this place had loads of security and you couldn't get past it all last time.'

'We couldn't,' Jack said. 'But there aren't any guards in the building, right?'

'Yeah,' Talya said.

'And Hector's people are in there. Yes?' Jack said.

She nodded.

'So the place isn't on total lockdown.' Jack pointed at the main doors. 'You just need to get us through those when I say so.'

'Outside cameras are now off,' Slink whispered.

'OK,' Jack said to Talya. 'You're up.'

Talya nodded at Skin.

He pressed a phone to his ear. 'Go.'

And Jack's eyes went wide as hundreds of kids came running down the road towards them.

CHAPTER EIGHT

TALYA'S GANG RAN DOWN THE ROAD, SCREAMING and brandishing clubs and weapons.

Jack thought it was both an impressive and terrifying thing to witness.

Talya looked at Jack with a smug expression. 'Why d'ya look so shocked?'

Jack made a show of straightening his face. 'I just wasn't expecting so many of them.'

'What were you expecting?' Talya said, apparently amused.

'I dunno,' Jack said. 'Maybe, like, ten or twenty extra people to help us out.'

The kids reached the front of the Millbarn building and started smashing the glass doors and windows.

'Not very subtle, are they?' Charlie said.

'Jacky didn't want subtle,' Talya retorted. 'Did ya?'

Jack chose not to answer her.

With the main door now smashed and torn from its frame, Talya's gang poured through the front of the building.

'Time to go,' Talya said, wheeling herself towards the mayhem.

Jack, Charlie, Wren, Skin and the others followed.

Once inside, the crowd parted, letting them through.

Talya stopped in the middle of the foyer, the smirk on her face bigger than ever.

Jack was determined to wipe that away. But he had to be patient and play it carefully. Talya was predictable, but also temperamental and dangerous. Jack knew he had to adapt this mission as it went along.

'Skin?' Talya said, as more of her gang forced their way into the building.

Skin cleared his throat and stepped forward. He held up his hands and shouted, 'All right, you bunch of freaks. Shut up.'

If Hector's men hadn't noticed hundreds of kids flooding into the building already, then the shouting would certainly draw their attention – which, for once, was exactly what Jack wanted to happen.

'I said, shut up,' Skin bellowed.

The kids quieted down and turned to look at him and Talya.

'OK, Skin,' Talya said in a calm voice. 'Now you have their attention...' She glanced at Jack and winked. 'You're gonna like this next bit.'

'Right then,' Skin called to the group. 'You know what to do, so get on with it.'

The entire gang of kids roared and streamed towards the stairs.

'Wait.' Jack spun to Talya. 'They're only supposed to guard the exits and stop anyone leaving. What are you doing?'

'It's OK, Jacky boy,' she said. 'They're just gonna sweep through the building and find this Hector kid for ya. Save ya some time, like.'

'Stop them,' Jack said. 'This isn't the plan.'

Jack knew Hector wouldn't be here, but he wasn't prepared to let Talya find that out. And God only knew what Hector's men would do if they were rushed by all these kids at once. And Obi *was* in there...

'You need to calm yourself,' Talya said with a crooked smile. 'Don't worry about it. My army have orders that when they find Hector and his mates they're not to move in on them until we get there.'

'Will they follow those orders?' Charlie asked, blowing her nose and watching the kids shove and push each other.

Talya followed her gaze and shrugged. 'I can't promise they won't do a little bit of criminal damage on their way.' She nodded at a couple of kids who were ripping a fire extinguisher from the wall. 'But they'll get the job done.'

'Why don't you just follow the plan?' Wren said.

Talya's expression hardened to stone. 'Because I don't trust any of you. That's why.'

As the foyer cleared, Jack took the walkie-talkie from Charlie and pressed it to his ear. 'Slink?'

'I'm in the main security room,' Slink said. 'I had to pick the lock, just like you thought. There's no one in here though, which is good.'

Jack let out a slow breath. At least one thing was going the way he'd hoped. 'Any sign of movement?'

'What?' Slink said. 'You mean apart from the million hooligans barrelling up the stairs?'

'Yeah,' Jack said, glancing at Talya. 'Apart from that.'

'Nothing,' Slink said. 'The cameras only cover the corridors, but so far I haven't seen anyone else.'

For a fleeting moment, Jack's stomach tightened. What if Hector's men had moved Obi out of the building already?

'What about remote viewers?' he asked.

'I haven't found any extra wires connected to the security system yet,' Slink replied. 'Need some help.'

'OK,' Jack said. 'I'm sending Wren to you. She'll help look.' He nodded at her and she hurried off.

Jack felt bad, but with Talya around, he just needed to keep the Outlaws as safe as possible. By sending Wren away to help Slink, they'd both stand a good chance at getting out if the mission went wrong.

'Keep us updated,' Jack said to Slink.

'Wren and me will keep an eye out,' Slink said. 'We've got this covered.'

'Thanks.' Jack handed the walkie-talkie back to Charlie, and started pacing.

He wondered if all this might be one of Hector's traps, but then Jack reminded himself that Connor hadn't realised they'd followed him from the bunker earlier. Jack allowed that thought to relax him slightly.

But the relief was short-lived because the next few minutes passed like an hour. The longer they waited, the tighter his chest felt. The anxiety mixed with the virus meant he was finding it very hard to breathe.

Charlie sneezed and then promptly went into a coughing fit.

Skin slapped her on the back. 'There, there, princess.'

'Get off me,' Charlie growled.

'You lot look worse by the second,' Talya said, seeming happy about that. 'You are gonna make it, ain't ya?'

Jack ground his teeth. Obi's life rested on them not messing up and he wanted to get this over with as quickly as possible.

Talya's phone rang, and all eyes moved to her as she answered.

'Yeah?' She listened for a moment. 'Right.' She hung up and looked at Jack. 'Tenth floor. Just like you thought. Rest of the building is empty.' She wheeled herself towards the lift. 'Come with me.'

Jack glanced at Charlie and together they hurried after her.

The lift doors opened and Jack, Charlie, Talya and Skin went inside.

Skin hit the tenth-floor button, the doors closed and the lift ascended.

They stood in silence for several moments as music played in the background.

It was absurd, Jack thought. Here they were, in the middle of a dangerous mission, with hundreds of kids cornering Hector's men, and the four of them were listening to classical music that sounded like it was being played on milk bottles.

The lift stopped, and Jack, Charlie and Skin followed Talya into the hallway.

It was packed full of kids and they stood aside to let them through.

At the far end of the hallway, Talya paused outside a door and looked up at one of her gang members, a kid with short-cropped hair and a crooked nose with a ring through it.

'Well?' Talya asked her in a low voice.

'They're in there,' the girl said, nodding at the door.

'How many?'

'Not sure.' The girl sniffed. 'I reckon at least two.'

'At least two?' Talya said, keeping her voice low and measured. 'If you're not sure, why d'you think there's at least two in there then?'

The girl visibly tensed. 'I didn't get a good look.' She pointed down the hallway. 'We were searching rooms. I was about to check this one when the door slammed shut and they locked it from the inside.' She glanced uneasily at Skin. 'I saw two of them – one big guy, and a fat bloke sitting in a chair, facing away from the door.'

Jack looked at Charlie. Neither of them needed to say anything.

'There's only two geezers in there?' Talya said to Jack. 'Strange.' Her eyes narrowed. 'Where are the others? Where's Hector?'

'No idea.' Jack glanced back down the hallway. 'Tell your army to search the building again.'

Talya stared at him. 'There had better be a juicy set of mission plans in there, Jack. Otherwise I'm killing all of ya, right here and now. Understood?'

Jack nodded.

Talya waved off the girl, then nodded at Skin. 'Break the door down.'

'No,' Jack said, grabbing Skin's arm.

Skin glared at him. 'Get off me before I headbutt ya.'

'But we don't know what's on the other side of the door,' Jack persisted. 'There could be ten of them in there for all we know, each one armed.' He gestured at the girl. 'She only saw two men, but there could

172

be more in there. We don't know for sure that they're alone.'

'I don't care about weapons.' Talya was accustomed to using the brute force method in all her plans.

'What do you think will happen if you go storming in there?' Jack said. 'They'll destroy the plans.'

This caused a flicker of hesitation to cross Talya's face.

Jack remained silent, watching her.

Talya looked at the door for a long moment, then her eyes slowly moved back to him. 'What do you suggest then?'

Jack stared at the ceiling and quickly thought it through, visualising the layout of the Millbarn building.

'OK,' he said in a hushed voice, looking at Talya again. 'I do have an idea.'

Talya leant forward in her chair. 'Spill it.'

Jack swallowed. The trick that would get Obi out of that room rested on the hope that Hector's men had indeed tapped into the building's CCTV cameras and were watching them right at that very moment. In fact, he'd bet that was the reason they wouldn't answer the door.

Jack glanced around at all the kids cramming the hallway and offices then looked back at Talya. 'Right. I need this whole floor empty. Send your gang to the floor above and tell them to pretend to search the rooms.'

Talya's eyes narrowed to slits. 'And why would I do that?'

Jack lowered his voice further. 'Because we need them to know there's no one on this level.'

'Why?'

'Trust me,' Jack said.

Talya snorted. 'Not a chance. You think I'm stupid? I'm not falling for your cons any more, Jack. You tell me why first. Then I'll decide if I agree to it or not.'

'They're watching the security cameras.' Jack nodded at one over his shoulder. 'They'll be able to see us right now.'

'So what?'

'We need them to see everyone leave,' Jack said, trying to control his temper – Talya was beginning to really irritate him. 'Then they'll feel safe enough to come out when we give them a good reason to.' He leant forward until his face was a couple of milli-metres from hers and whispered, 'We need them to change offices.'

Talya stared at him for a long moment, then her eyes widened. 'That's quite clever.' She grinned, revealing crooked teeth.

Jack straightened up. 'Thanks.'

'All right, Jack, we'll try it your way. But...' Talya pointed a finger at him, 'you make a single false step, and I'll 'ave you hung out of a window. Understood?' She looked at Skin. 'Give him whatever he wants.'

Skin's eyes narrowed, but, as always, he obviously knew better than to argue with her.

Jack turned to Charlie. 'Can you find something to lock the doors with?'

Charlie glanced at the locks. 'Yes.'

'Good,' Jack said. 'Do it.'

Charlie entered a couple of offices and returned a few minutes later with several paper clips, a small knife and a letter opener.

Jack looked between her and Skin. 'Follow me.'

He walked down the corridor and asked Charlie to lock each of the doors after he checked inside the offices. Jack also made sure that several kids stood between her and the security cameras, blocking the view of what Charlie was doing.

Jack finally found an office that was suitable for their needs – the CCTV camera at the end of the hall had a clear view inside it. Once Charlie had finished locking every other door in the hallway, they went in.

There was a group of kids playing a game on a computer – a MMORPG called *Sky Attack!*, involving aliens and lots of guns.

'We need this place emptied,' Jack said to Skin.

For a moment, Skin looked like he was going to refuse to help, but he turned to the room and said, 'Everyone out.'

The kids looked up at him.

'*Now*,' he shouted.

The kids jumped to their feet and filed from the room.

Once it was empty, Jack could see that on the right-hand wall there was a large bookcase next to a door that led to a kitchenette.

Jack examined the door's hinges. 'We need to unscrew these.'

'JP, get 'ere,' Skin shouted into the hallway.

Five seconds later, a kid with red hair and freckles walked into the office. He was wearing a large back-pack that a hiker or camper might use. 'What?'

Skin spun him around, rummaged through the backpack then pulled out a crowbar.

Jack thought about stopping him, but decided that Skin's way was probably quicker than trying to unscrew each hinge.

There was a cracking of wood as Skin set to work and in under a minute he was done. He returned the crowbar to JP's bag and sent him away.

'Thanks.' Jack coughed and winced.

Skin scowled at him.

Jack stepped to the bookcase next to the door and started removing books from the lower shelves and putting them on higher ones.

'What are you doing?' Skin asked, with a look of confusion.

Jack reached up and rocked the bookcase backwards and forwards. Satisfied it was now top-heavy, he stepped past Skin, back into the hallway and over to Talya.

'We're ready.' He then explained what he wanted Talya's army to do next.

Talya nodded. 'For your sake, Jack, I hope this works.'

'Me too.'

Together, they returned to the office.

Jack lifted the kitchenette door aside, then he turned back to Talya. 'Make sure everyone leaves at the same time. That way, Hector's men will think Charlie and I have left too.'

'Yeah, yeah, I get it.' Talya looked over at Skin. 'Tell everyone that when we leave the office, they all get out of 'ere at the same time, just like Jack says – clear the entire floor. Then go upstairs and search it. Every room. Right?'

'And make sure you leave a few people in the exit stairwell on both the floor above and below,' Jack said. 'So Hector's men don't slip past us.'

Skin glared at him, then spun around and marched into the corridor to give the orders.

'Get in here, you two,' Talya said to a couple of kids standing just outside the door. One was tall and wearing a baseball cap; the other had bright blue hair.

They entered the office and Talya's gaze moved back to Jack. 'What about the lifts?'

'You go up a floor in the first one,' Jack said. 'Then jam the door open so it's stuck up there. Once we give the all-clear, you can come back down in another lift. The stairs and lifts will be covered by your people, so there's no escape.' He turned to Charlie. 'Please disable the second lift,' he said with a hard look, hoping she understood his meaning.

Charlie nodded and hurried from the office.

Skin returned. 'Everyone's ready an' knows what to do.'

'You'll need weapons,' Talya said to Jack. She reached down the side of her chair, pulled out two black cans and handed them to him.

'Pepper spray?' Jack's eyebrows lifted. He wasn't sure if he was surprised that Talya had them hidden on her or not.

Talya grinned. 'You can never be too careful, can ya?'

Charlie returned and Jack stepped into the kitchenette with her.

'Put the bookcase in front of the doorway,' he said to Skin.

'You'd better get me those plans, Jack,' Talya warned.

Jack returned her cold stare as Skin and the other two kids slid the bookcase in front of the door frame. Then it all went quiet.

Jack handed a can of pepper spray to Charlie.

'Wanna explain what's going on then?' she said.

'Hector's not in that office with Obi.'

'Yeah, well, I know that,' Charlie said. 'And I think Talya knows that too.'

'It doesn't matter if she does,' Jack said, keeping his voice low. 'All Talya is after is mission plans.'

'But what if there are loads of Hector's men in there?'

'I think it's just Monday.'

'How can you be so sure?'

'I'm not. But remember when we first scoped out that room, back on the Richard Hardy mission?'

Charlie nodded.

'The office is fairly small and when the door's open you have a clear view of the entire room. I'm guessing that girl would've seen if anyone else was in there.'

'So, what's going on now?' Charlie asked.

'One of Talya's gang is going to set a small fire and shove it under the door.'

Charlie's mouth dropped open. 'What?'

'It's OK.' Jack pointed above their heads to the sprinkler. 'There's one in each room. I just need Monday to change offices to this one.'

Jack gestured for the walkie-talkie. She handed it to him and Jack brought Slink up to speed with what he wanted to happen.

'That wasn't part of the original mission,' Slink said when he'd finished.

'Since when have we ever been able to stick to Plan A?' Jack asked him.

'Yeah,' Slink said. 'Actually, that's a really good point. Maybe when you next come up with mission ideas, you should make your first plan Plan B and your second one Plan A. That way we don't have to keep changing mid-mission, like a bunch of idiots.' He sneezed, as if adding an exclamation mark to his suggestion.

'I'll take that on board,' Jack muttered, rolling his eyes at Charlie as she grinned at him. 'So,' Jack continued in a low voice, 'do you understand what you need to do?'

'Of course,' Slink said.

'And what do you see on the cameras?' Jack asked.

'Talya's doing like you said – she's up on the next floor and has jammed open the lift. The only other way out of there is the stairs.'

'Good,' Jack said.

For once, Talya was doing something the way he wanted it done.

'And some little kid with long blond hair has started a fire. He's running back to the others.'

Jack held his breath.

'Well,' Charlie said, leaning against a countertop. 'If that doesn't make Monday panic, nothing will.'

'What's happening now?' Jack asked Slink.

'No movement on your floor yet. Wait,' he said. 'Now there is – the door just opened.'

'Who is it?'

There was a short pause. 'Monday. And he's got Obi tied to an office chair. Gagged too.'

Jack glanced at Charlie and fought the urge to break out of the room and rescue Obi now. Any false moves and the mission could end in disaster.

'Anyone else?' he asked.

'Can't see anyone,' Slink said.

Jack let out a breath.

'Monday's stamping out the flames. There's a lot of smoke. Wait. Hold on. Monday's coming your way. He's dragging Obi with him and checking doors. They're all locked.'

A few seconds later, Jack heard the office door open.

'Monday's going in,' Slink said.

'With Obi?'

'He's left Obi by the door and is checking out the office.'

Jack grabbed the pepper spray. 'Ready?' he whispered to Charlie.

She nodded, held up her can and braced herself.

Jack shouldered the bookcase, sending it crashing into the room.

Monday spun to face them, but Charlie and Jack raised their cans high and sprayed him in the face. Monday staggered backwards and fell over the desk.

Jack continued forwards, following him with the spray, unleashing the can's contents into his face. Monday's arms flailed about and he groaned as his eyes streamed.

'Quick,' Jack shouted, throwing the can aside. He gripped the back of Obi's chair and dragged him into the hallway.

Charlie threw her own can at Monday then ran after Jack and slammed the door shut.

Together they dragged Obi up the hallway and into the second lift.

Charlie reached behind the control panel and joined two wires, and the lights came back on.

'Ground floor,' Jack said.

She hit the button and the doors closed.

They then hurried to untie Obi.

Obi flexed his neck and arms. 'Thought you were never gonna rescue me.' His voice came out as a croaky whisper and he looked deathly pale.

'Are you OK?' Jack said.

'No. Feel horrible.'

'We do too,' Jack said. 'Where's Connor?'

Obi rubbed his wrists. 'He left about an hour ago.'

Jack swore to himself. One of them should've been watching the building.

But there was no time for 'what ifs'. They needed to get out before Talya caught up with them.

The lift doors opened and Jack helped Obi to his feet.

'Time to wrap this up,' Jack said.

Jack, Charlie and Obi stepped out into the lobby to find Slink and Wren were waiting for them.

'We've got a slight problem,' Slink said. 'We couldn't follow your plan exactly.'

Jack's stomach sank. 'Why not?'

'The security computer has just locked us out,' Slink said. 'It detected a fire and went into emergency mode. It needs an administrator password.'

Jack pinched the bridge of his nose. 'I can deal with it. Meet me outside.'

They all hesitated.

Jack lowered his hand. 'Go.'

Slink, Obi and Wren ran for the main doors.

Charlie stayed put.

'I said go,' Jack told her. 'Leave.'

'Are you sure? We can just leg it.'

Jack glanced back at the stairs as he heard hundreds of feet running down them. 'It's the only way. Otherwise she'll keep coming after us.'

Charlie gave him a curt nod. 'Try and get out in one piece.'

She ran after the others through the main doors.

Jack turned on his heels, sprinted down the corridor and burst into the security room. He dropped into the seat and his eyes flittered over the screens.

He could see Talya's army running down the stairs, each with a look of pure rage on their face.

Jack had seconds to solve this problem.

He swore and looked at the password box on the main screen. There just wasn't enough time to hack it.

Jack slammed his fists on to the desk. 'Think.' He stared at the blinking cursor. '*Think*,' he growled.

It came to him in a flash. If the main computer failed, the building's security would go into full automatic lockdown.

He glanced at Talya's gang still sprinting down the stairs and hoped the programmed time delay wouldn't last too long.

Not wasting a microsecond more, Jack reached around the back of the main security computer, grabbed the power cable and yanked it out.

A high-pitched ringing blared out from the alarm box on the wall.

Jack leapt to his feet, burst into the corridor and ran into the foyer, just as Talya wheeled herself out of one of the lifts, with Skin close behind.

Skin's eyes locked on to Jack and he squeezed past her. 'I'm gonna kill him.'

Jack glanced to his left.

Steel shutters were rolling down the outside of the Millbarn building. At the same time, hundreds of Talya's gang ran down the stairs and erupted into the foyer.

Head low, Jack sprinted towards the main doors.

Talya screamed, '*Jack!*'

Skin roared and ran after Jack, with the gang surging behind him.

Jack hit the floor, slid across the shattered glass and squeezed under the steel shutters just in time.

He heard hundreds of bodies slam into the other side.

Jack rolled on to his back and looked up, breathing heavily, wincing from the pain in his chest.

'Er, Jack,' Slink called.

He looked over.

Slink pointed.

Further down the road – and marching towards them – were six men in army uniform carrying automatic weapons.

Jack groaned. 'They're early.'

CHAPTER NINE

CHARLIE HELPED JACK TO HIS FEET AND BRUSHED glass from his clothes. 'What do you mean, they're early?'

The six army men continued marching towards the Outlaws. In the distance, what seemed like a thousand blue flashing lights lit up the sky and their sirens grew louder with every passing moment.

'What have you done now?' Slink said.

'Not me,' Jack said. 'Noble.' He gestured at the army men. 'I asked him to call them.'

'Why on Earth would you do that?' Charlie asked, her eyes wide.

Jack motioned for Obi and Wren to stay close. 'To collect our friends inside.' Jack took a step forward and held up his hands. 'Officers, there's been a break-in,' he called, trying to look innocent. 'We'll get out of your way.'

Jack went to step aside, but the leader raised his gun.

'You'll stay right there.'

'Great plan, Jack,' Slink muttered. 'What now?'

'Now?' Jack let out a laboured breath. 'Now, I guess we have to run.'

Charlie and Wren groaned.

'You've got to be kidding,' Obi said.

'Please tell me your plan allowed for this problem?' Charlie hissed through the corner of her mouth.

Now only ten metres away, the other men raised their guns too.

'Hands in the air.'

Suddenly, a head popped up from a manhole cover between the Outlaws and the men, and Raze launched an object the size of a hand grenade at the army men.

It rolled along the ground and stopped a metre or so in front of them.

The lead man looked down at it, then his eyes locked on to the smoke issuing from one end. 'Cover,' he shouted.

A split second later, the homemade bomb exploded in a blinding flash and a huge ball of smoke erupted into the air.

The lead army man dived, but the others were too slow – they staggered backwards, shielding their eyes.

Three more heads appeared from behind a wall to their left – Domino, Wilf and Ryan – and they too threw homemade bombs at them then disappeared.

Jack looked into the distance as several police cars slid into the road. 'Time to go,' he said.

The Outlaws took off in the opposite direction as the bombs exploded behind them.

The lead army man shouted commands.

Jack glanced back to see him grab the man nearest to him by the jacket collar and thrust him forward.

The man raised his gun to his shoulder and a shot rang out.

Jack ducked as brickwork above his head shattered, showering him in splinters and chunks of debris.

Keeping his head low, Jack raced around the corner of the building and pelted after the others.

'Guess that answers my question,' Charlie called over her shoulder as they skirted the rear of the Millbarn building and darted down an alleyway.

'What question's that?' Jack shouted back at her, clutching his chest and struggling to breathe.

'They'll definitely shoot kids.'

Jack wasn't so sure. Anyone in the army would no doubt have an accurate shot – he must have missed on purpose. But Jack didn't want to stick around long enough to test that theory out.

The Outlaws reached a gate at the end of the alley. Slink threw it open, and the five of them rushed through, across a road and between two buildings.

'Guys, do we have to go so fast?' Obi wheezed as his feet pounded the tarmac. 'I'm gonna throw up.'

'Me too,' Wren said. 'My muscles are killing me.'

Slink forced a grin at her. 'What muscles?'

Another shot rang out, making them all duck.

'What was that you were asking, Obi?' Slink said, darting between a fence and a wall.

Another shot rang out, but the Outlaws were already in motion, heading towards Blandford Road and the nearest entrance to the tunnels that led to the cavern.

Once safely back at the cavern, the Outlaws dropped next to the firepit, exhausted, while Raze, Wilf, Ryan and Domino grabbed cans of drink for everyone and sat with them.

'That was fun,' Raze said, gulping lemonade and sniffing.

'Yeah,' said Ryan, his eyes wide. 'If you guys do that sort of thing all the time then tell me how I join your gang.'

'That sort of thing doesn't always go exactly to plan though.' Jack smiled, then coughed and winced. The pain in his chest was still getting worse and he was finding it harder to breathe.

'If Jack had his way,' Slink said, taking off his trainers and flexing his toes, 'he'd be in the bunker with a hot-water bottle and a fluffy blanket.'

Everyone chuckled.

'I'd actually quite like a hot-water bottle and a blanket right about now,' Wren said, hugging herself.

'Erm, Jack?' Obi said in a small voice.

'Yeah?'

'It's gone.'

Jack frowned at him. 'What has?'

'The bunker. They set fire to the whole place.'

Jack slouched forward.

'It can't all be gone,' Charlie said, looking absolutely devastated.

Jack could see that, like him, she must have hoped they'd be able to sneak back and retrieve at least some of their belongings.

'It's gone, Charlie,' Obi said. 'All of it. I watched them torch it after they snatched me.'

'But Connor went back there,' Slink said.

'I know,' Obi said. 'When he got Jack's message and saw the IP address was coming from the bunker, Hector thought they hadn't done their job properly. So Connor went to check.'

Jack shook his head.

All gone, he thought. *All of it.*

The door at the far end of the cavern opened and Noble walked in carrying several shopping bags.

'I managed to find us some supplies,' he said brightly. He set the bags down, spotted Obi and grinned. 'I'm so glad you're back safe.' Noble pulled out cans of soup and loaves of bread. 'Did everything go OK?'

'Yeah,' Obi said, turning to Jack. 'Can you explain what just happened?'

Jack shifted his weight and cricked his neck. 'I thought it would be a good opportunity to combine two missions. One: save you. Two: get rid of Talya once and for all.'

'She's trapped in that building, right?' Wren said. 'And her gang too?'

Jack nodded. 'That's not all.' He gestured to Noble.

'I suggested that the authorities should investigate Talya's warehouse as soon as they're able to,' Noble added. 'With all those stolen goods she's got there, I don't expect we'll be seeing her or Skin again anytime soon.'

Charlie, Obi, Slink and Wren were silent for a few moments, then all four of them burst out laughing.

'That's brilliant, Jack,' Obi said. 'Absolutely brilliant.'

'That'll get Talya back for Scarlett,' Wren said.

Charlie smiled at Jack and winked.

It was true, Jack thought – he did feel a little better now that Talya had got her comeuppance. Although of course it would never completely make up for Scarlett and it definitely wouldn't bring her back.

Obi looked over at Noble and frowned. He was unpacking several cans of tinned vegetables.

'Where did you get all that food?' Wren asked.

'Certainly not the supermarkets,' Noble said. 'It's pandemonium up there.'

'We noticed that on our way back here,' Domino said. 'People have lost the plot, if you ask me. They're looting and all sorts.'

Noble walked over and handed a netbook to Jack.

'Thank you,' Jack said, surprised.

Noble sat down by the fire with a heavy sigh. 'It's the best I could get.'

'It's perfect,' Jack said. 'Where did you get it?'

'The same place as the food.' Noble warmed his hands and looked at Jack, Charlie and Obi. 'Do you recall our friend Abdul?'

They nodded.

'Who's Abdul?' Slink asked.

'Before your time,' Charlie said.

'It was one of the early missions,' Obi said to Slink. 'We hadn't met you yet. Abdul was being blackmailed by a local gang and we helped him out.'

'Abdul's never forgotten us,' Noble added. 'Or what we did for him.' He nodded at the bags. 'No matter what happens to us, we'll never go hungry.'

'Abdul's shop hasn't been raided then?' Jack asked.

'Yes,' Noble said. 'But he moved all his stock to the lock-up behind the main building. They won't be getting at that in a hurry.'

'Why hasn't this Abdul guy got out of London?' Wilf asked.

The corners of Noble's lips twitched. 'He says the day he leaves London is the day hell freezes over and we can all go ice skating.'

Jack wondered how many other people had refused to leave. London was a huge city and there were literally millions of places to hide – evacuating every single person would be an impossible task.

He watched the flames and also pondered how different life would've been if Hector's dad hadn't found out the location of the bunker. Would all this mess have been over by now? He strongly suspected the answer to that was *yes*.

Noble let out a long breath. 'Obi, any intel on Hector's whereabouts?'

'I never saw him,' Obi said. 'It was just Monday and Connor there.'

'He obviously thought it was too risky taking you to his hideout.' Noble turned to Jack. 'Hector's not as stupid as first thought.'

'Hector's definitely not stupid,' Jack said. 'We've learnt that the hard way. Which is why this is such a nightmare now.'

Slink snorted. 'You're cleverer than that bozo any day of the week, Jack.'

'Thanks.'

'Now Obi's been rescued, won't that Connor guy be going back to Hector's hideout?' Domino asked.

'Yeah,' Ryan said. 'You could've put a tracker on his car.'

'We don't have a bunker,' Jack said. 'Which also means we don't have a tracker or any way to follow it.'

'Well, that is a slight problem,' Raze muttered.

'We do have a plan though,' Jack continued. 'Trouble is, we're struggling to find a fast internet connection in order for me to activate my tracer program and find where Trent Myer lives. If I can get to him, I can find Hector's IP.'

'The internet isn't working too well,' Ryan said. 'It hasn't been since they started evacuating the city.'

Noble got to his feet. 'I think I may know of one place that still has a fast connection.'

Jack frowned for a moment then he understood what Noble had in mind. 'Oh no. Please, anywhere but there.'

'There is nowhere else,' Noble said. 'The rest of London is shutting down. It's the only place I can think of that will still have a functional, fast and reliable internet connection.'

Jack shook his head, but he couldn't think of an alternative. 'So, how are we going to do it with no equipment?'

Noble stared into space for a moment. 'The old-fashioned way, I suppose – using our heads.'

Jack glanced around. All the others had puzzled expressions.

'Do what?' Charlie asked. 'What are we doing exactly?'

Jack stood beside Charlie and Noble in front of a metal door at the foot of a tall concrete building. His eyes moved upwards, following a circular tower as it stretched high above him. About two-thirds of the way up, the tower's construction was partly open to the elements and there were several satellite dishes and antennae mounted to the framework.

The BT Tower was one of the most recognisable landmarks in London, and would have the best chance of an uninterrupted and fast internet connection.

Noble handed Jack a phone and headset. 'Take these.'

'Where are they from?'

'Abdul. He gave them to me along with the net-book. My number is in the contacts list.'

Jack stared at him a moment. He had a strange feeling he knew what Noble was planning. Jack opened his mouth to ask, but Noble stepped to the door.

'Keep a lookout please, Charlie.' Noble folded the lapel of his coat over, revealing a hidden compartment of lock picks. He selected the appropriate one, then set to work on the door.

Jack counted in his head and he'd just got to twenty seconds when the lock clicked.

Noble straightened up and turned to Jack and Charlie. 'I can do something about the cameras, but not the alarm,' he said. 'We need to act fast.'

Jack nodded and checked the netbook was still secure in the backpack he had slung over his shoulder.

Noble opened the door, and Jack and Charlie quickly followed him inside.

Noble stopped, held up a hand and pointed at the camera above his head. It was aiming down the corridor and would easily spot them.

Standing directly under it, Noble removed his watch. He twiddled the dial then reached up and wedged the watch behind the CCTV camera.

'Stand back.'

The three of them edged back to the door and stared up at it.

A few seconds later, there was a huge electrical spark from the watch and the camera light went out.

Charlie grinned. 'Did that just electrocute the camera's circuits?'

'Twenty thousand volts.' Noble reached up and retrieved his watch. 'One of Serene's acquisitions. She tells me that both the American and British secret services use them – I dread to think what for. I'm amazed she got it through customs.'

Jack couldn't help but smile too. Noble and his sister Serene loved their high-tech gadgets. 'Can it tell the time though?' he asked.

Noble looked at the display. 'Apparently not any more, no.'

The three of them jogged down a couple of hallways, through unmarked doors, then eventually came out at a lift.

Noble hit the up arrow, the doors opened, and they rushed inside.

As the doors slid closed, Jack swallowed. 'How high are we going?'

'The tower's one hundred and eighty-nine metres tall, if I remember correctly,' Noble said. 'Although we won't be going quite that far.'

Jack let out a breath. 'Good.' He wasn't sure if he was shaking from the virus or his fear of heights.

Noble pressed a button on the lift panel and Jack's stomach flipped as it ascended.

A woman's disembodied voice said, 'The lift is now travelling at one thousand, four hundred feet per minute.'

Jack watched the screen above the door count the floors.

The lift slowed.

'Thirty-fourth floor.'

'Get ready,' Noble said. 'We have no way of knowing if we'll have company up here.'

'Doors opening.'

Jack braced himself, though there was nothing but a darkened space beyond.

Cautiously, the three of them crept out and looked about.

The entire level was an observation deck with windows floor to ceiling. The view over London was impressive, but Jack's vertigo held him back from taking a closer look.

He glanced left and right. There were chairs, benches and tables, but no people.

'Well,' Noble said, 'that's definitely a plus side to London being evacuated – very few people around.'

He strode around the corner to another door, and Jack and Charlie followed.

Noble picked the lock and stepped to one side. 'You're on your own from here.' He handed Charlie the set of lock picks. 'In case you need them.'

Jack frowned at Noble. 'Why aren't you coming with us?'

'We triggered a back-to-base alarm when we entered.' Noble gave him a half-hearted smile. 'They'll be expecting to catch someone up here and it'll be better if it's me.' He took several backward steps and peered around the corner. 'That was quicker than I expected. Looks like they're on their way up here now.'

'You knew this would happen, didn't you?' Charlie said. 'You've sacrificed yourself.'

'No,' Jack said. 'Noble, we can't let you do this.'

Noble rested hands on both their shoulders. 'Find Hector. That's your priority right now. Getting to that antidote is all that matters.' He leant forward and fixed Jack with a serious expression. 'I believe in you, Jack. I believe in all of you. The five of you can do this on your own. You don't need me any more.'

Jack opened his mouth to answer, but no words formed. He felt like they would always need Noble. He was their mentor and they owed him everything.

They heard the sound of the lift opening and then torch beams bounced around the walls.

Noble opened the door and gestured. 'Go,' he breathed.

Reluctantly, Jack followed Charlie through.

He turned back just in time to see the door close again and hear a muffled voice say, 'Hands up.'

CHAPTER TEN

JACK STARED AT THE CLOSED DOOR AND HEARD Noble say, 'No need for guns, gentlemen. You've caught me. I shall come along quietly.'

Charlie grabbed Jack's arm. 'Hurry,' she whispered in his ear, and gestured to another door. 'There's nothing we can do for him.'

'He's sacrificed himself,' Jack breathed.

'You would've done the same.'

Jack looked at her. Charlie was right – he would, but that didn't make it any easier to abandon Noble.

Then Jack felt his pocket for the phone Noble had given him and thought about how careful Noble had been to tell him that his phone number was in the contacts list.

And then he understood.

'He wants them to take him,' Jack said.

Charlie frowned. 'What do you mean?'

He handed her the phone. 'Look after this. I'll explain later.' Jack forced himself to turn from the door. 'Come on,' he whispered.

They sneaked through the other door, bolted it, then together they hurried up a set of metal stairs.

At the top, Jack and Charlie jogged right and into a small server room with rows of cabinets. Against one wall was a desk with a computer.

Jack sat in front of it and shook the mouse, but, as he'd predicted, it needed a password and he didn't want to waste time hacking it. Instead Jack slipped the netbook out of his bag and opened it. The screen sprang to life. He took the network cable out of the computer and plugged it into the netbook.

Jack took a breath then got to work. First, he logged into the Cerberus forum, navigated to his personal folder and found the app that would locate the tracer program he'd planted on Raze's laptop.

Jack hesitated, his finger hovering over the Enter button.

'What's the matter?' Charlie hissed.

Jack cricked his neck and tried to clear his mind. He had a headache and his vision was blurring. He blinked and concentrated the best he could, but the virus was really and truly getting to him now.

He just needed to think this through a moment.

Trent Myer's home network would be less secure than Cerberus, but it would still be formidable. Jack would have to move fast – as soon as the tracer returned a signal, revealing where it was, he had to get into Trent Myer's home network and out again before Trent realised what was happening.

Jack focused on the display and his finger landed on the Enter button.

The app sent out a signal, looking for the tracer program, and he held his breath.

Thirty seconds later, it returned a result.

'Got it.' Jack opened a command prompt and followed the route back to Trent's personal network.

It had several firewalls and programs monitoring traffic, but, one by one, Jack managed to override them all.

There was a muffled thud, along with shouting.

Charlie whirled around. 'They've just found the locked door downstairs. They've realised we're up here.'

Jack continued to type, his fingers and subconscious working as one.

Next came a loud crashing noise.

'Quick, Jack,' Charlie said. 'They've broken through.'

'I need another minute.'

He concentrated on the last firewall.

There were voices from the stairs.

'You really don't have a minute,' Charlie hissed.

Jack ignored her and willed his fingers to move as quickly as possible.

There were footfalls now, growing louder.

Charlie stepped to the door and locked it.

'Find an alternative way out,' Jack said, not taking his eyes off the netbook's screen.

He heard Charlie run to the back of the room and open another door.

Jack's fingers raced over the keyboard as he typed several commands and lines of code.

The door handle rattled.

Jack managed to get past the final firewall and he scanned Trent's computer logs. He frowned. 'Where is it?' he said under his breath.

Charlie returned. 'What are you doing?'

Someone banged on the door.

Charlie grabbed Jack's arm. 'We need to go. *Now.*'

Jack shrugged her off, and his eyes scanned the pages as his heart sank. 'Oh no.'

'What's wrong?'

Jack sat back. Trent had hidden his IP address, which meant they had no way to track down his house. Unless – a sudden thought struck him – the laptop itself showed a traceable IP. His fingers raced over the keyboard.

'Bingo,' Jack said. 'Got it.' He brought up a map, transferred the details and a blue dot appeared on the screen. He pointed. 'That's where Trent lives. We've got him.' Jack looked at Charlie. 'Did you find another way out of here?'

'Yeah, I've found a way,' Charlie said. 'But you're really not gonna like it.'

Jack groaned when he saw the look on her face and he stood up. 'What?'

There was a loud bang as something heavy slammed into the door and the frame started to split.

'Follow me,' Charlie said.

Jack disconnected the netbook and slipped it into his bag.

Together, they stepped into a smaller room and Charlie pointed at an open hatch above their heads. There was a metal ladder leading up.

A cold wind tore through the hatch and made Jack take an involuntary step backwards. 'You've got to be kidding me. Do you know how high up we are?'

There was another loud thud and the sound of more splitting wood.

'Not kidding,' Charlie said, racing up the ladder.

Muttering several swear words to himself, Jack clambered after her.

Once he was through, Charlie closed the hatch behind them, but there was no way to lock it from the outside.

They were now standing on a circular balcony with satellite and microwave dishes mounted to steel beams. Jack dared not take in the view before them as his vertigo would probably bring him to his knees.

'I've never seen London so dark,' Charlie said. 'There are hardly any lights on. No cars. No aeroplanes. Nothing. Jack, look at this – it's amazing.'

Jack kept his gaze firmly on his feet, pulled up his hood and coughed. 'I'll take your word for it.'

A scraping sound came from the other side of the hatch.

Charlie stepped to their right, ducked under a huge metal bracket and disappeared.

'Charlie?' Jack whispered.

He glanced back at the hatch. No doubt someone would come up there soon to investigate – and, as much as Jack hated to admit it, Charlie was probably right to hide.

Jack swallowed painfully as he looked at the metal beams and tried not to think about how high up they were. Why had Charlie picked a hiding place in such a terrifying –

Another sound came from below. This one sounded closer.

Jack glanced at the hatch one more time, regretting not finding somewhere else to hide down there where it was safe and warm. With huge reluctance, he ducked under the metal framework and popped up on the other side.

He looked around, but couldn't see Charlie.

'Hey,' her voice whispered.

He followed the sound of Charlie's voice. She was peering down from a platform above him.

'How did you get up there?' Jack asked.

Charlie pointed at the metal framework that jutted out from the building.

Jack shook his head. 'No way.'

There was the sound of the hatch banging open to their left, and Charlie ducked.

'Here,' she said, holding out a hand. 'Quick.'

Jack swore to himself, grabbed her hand for support and stepped up on to the metal beam.

'Hurry,' Charlie whispered. 'They're coming.'

Jack moved to the next beam and Charlie helped pull him up on to the platform. He'd just got his feet out of the way in time when a deep voice spoke.

'There must be someone up here. Both doors were locked from the inside.'

'There could be another way out we've missed,' a second voice said.

'I told you,' the first voice insisted. 'This is the only way. That old bloke wasn't alone.'

Jack stayed as still as possible, refusing to let Noble's sacrifice go to waste.

There was the rustling sound of fabric as the men climbed under the metalwork beneath them.

'There's no one up here,' the second voice said.

'I'm not leaving until we've searched every inch of this place.'

'Do what you want. I'm going back.'

Jack heard one set of heavy boots head in the direction of the hatch. He listened, but couldn't hear the other guy beneath them.

He imagined the man's narrowed eyes roaming over every nook and cranny, searching for any sign of intruders.

Jack's breath caught as he heard a heavy footstep on the frame below.

Charlie nudged him and they silently edged back.

A gloved hand appeared on the lip of the platform and Jack braced himself.

They were done for.

He looked about for an escape route, but they were trapped up there with nowhere to go.

The man grunted as he lifted himself and the top of his police helmet appeared a few centimetres in front of Jack's face.

Suddenly, a radio crackled.

'Now what?' the police officer snarled. He adjusted his weight. 'Go ahead.'

A faint voice said, 'The old man's given them up.'

'What do you mean?'

'He's taking us to the others now. They've already sneaked out of the tower and are hiding nearby.'

There was a long pause, then the police officer said, 'On my way.'

The helmet lowered back down.

Jack and Charlie let out simultaneous breaths and waited, listening as the man ducked under the framework and made his way down the hatch, closing it behind him.

Jack swung around and lowered himself to the balcony below, then he helped Charlie.

They crawled under the framework and hurried to the hatch.

Charlie grabbed the edge of the hatch and tried to lift it, but it didn't budge. 'Oh no.'

Jack stared down at her. 'You have got to be kidding me this time.'

Charlie grinned and opened the hatch. 'Yep.'

Jack clenched his teeth. 'Really *not* funny, Charlie. In fact, you're so far from funny that you're a speck on the horizon.'

Charlie descended the steps. 'Just thought it would spice things up a little.'

Jack rolled his eyes and followed her down. As they walked back through the server room, Jack stopped.

'What's wrong?' Charlie asked.

'Just a sec.' He went to the computer and grabbed a long network cable, then coiled it up and slipped it under his hoodie. 'OK, let's go.'

They quietly stepped to the door.

Charlie opened it a crack and peered out. 'I think they've gone,' she whispered.

They crept into the hallway, down the stairs, through the other door and back on to the observation lounge.

Charlie stopped at one of the windows and gasped.

'What's wrong now?' Jack asked.

She pointed.

In the distance, several buildings were on fire and huge flames erupted from their roofs.

Jack shook his head. 'This is insane.'

'We have to stop this madness,' Charlie said.

'I know,' Jack replied. 'We will.' He took her arm. 'Come on, we need to hurry.'

As they got into the lift, Charlie said, 'Where are we going?'

'Back to the cavern to get the others. We're going to need everyone's help to break into Trent Myer's house.'

As they left the BT Tower, Jack thought of what was to come. One more step, and they'd finally know where Hector was. One more obstacle, and they'd be on the home stretch.

An hour later, the five Outlaws were standing across the road from Trent Myer's terraced house in Kensington.

'I can see four cameras,' Obi said. 'And that's just on the front of the building. Want me to check the back?'

'The cameras aren't a problem,' Jack said, staring at the house.

'Why not?' Wren asked.

He glanced at her. 'Well, because of Hector, we're all famous. It makes no difference if we're caught on CCTV or not. Everyone knows who we are now anyway. No more hiding.' Jack looked up and down the road.

The fact that most people would know what the Outlaws looked like unnerved him. That was another thing Hector had taken from them – their anonymity.

For a fleeting moment, Jack worried about their future. If they did survive this, what then? Where would they live? What would they do? But these were questions for another day. Right now, they all had to focus on one task at a time and try to stay alive for as long as possible.

'What about the security alarm?' Charlie pointed to a box high up on the front wall of Trent's house.

'That's not really a problem either,' Jack said.

'Yeah, right,' Slink said. 'Like, who'd bother to come running if it went off? The police are a bit busy at the moment.' He hacked up phlegm and spat into the road.

Wren grimaced. 'That's disgusting.'

'Better than it being in my lungs,' Slink said. 'Well, what's left of them anyway.'

'The alarm on Trent's house won't be on,' Jack said, bringing the conversation back on track.

'Why not?' Obi asked.

'Because Trent is home. I guarantee it.'

Even though the house was in darkness, Jack just knew Trent would be in there. There was no way Trent would leave Cerberus unattended. But, if he wasn't, that meant they'd lost and it would be game over.

'OK,' Slink said, rubbing his hands together. 'How are we getting in then? By knocking on the front door?'

Charlie held up Noble's set of lock picks. 'With these.'

'He'll see us doing that on the cameras though,' Wren said.

Jack nodded. 'That's what we're counting on.'

They all looked at him.

Jack continued, 'Think it through. Trent runs Cerberus. Cerberus is world renowned as a place for all sorts of criminals to contact each other.'

'We're not criminals,' Wren said in a defensive tone.

'We are in the eyes of the law,' Charlie reminded her.

'And,' Jack continued, looking back at the house, 'Trent probably won't have any weapons to defend himself.'

'Why not?' Obi asked.

'Because he must be under permanent police surveillance. He knows that his nose needs to remain clean at all times, and injuring intruders, whoever they are, isn't going to keep the police on his side.'

Jack glanced up as smoke bellowed into the sky from a building on fire several roads away. In the distance, he could hear shouting and alarms.

'Wait a minute,' Obi said. 'What does Trent do if bad guys go after him? He doesn't have weapons to stop them, so that means he must have another way to defend himself.'

Jack gasped as he caught on. 'Why didn't I think of that sooner?'

'Think of what?' Charlie asked.

'No weapons,' Jack said. 'But Trent still needs some sort of defence.' He cleared his throat and winced. 'So,' he said in a hoarse voice, 'Trent's gotta have a panic room.'

A panic room was a secret room that you could seal yourself inside safely in case of an emergency.

It was a bit like a bank vault – once the door was closed, it was practically impossible to get through.

'Really?' Slink said.

Jack nodded. 'He must have. And I bet that if we walk up to his front door, he'll see us on the cameras, realise who we are and hide inside it.'

'And if we're quick,' Obi added, 'he won't have time to take his computer with him.'

'Right,' Charlie said, glancing between Jack and Obi. 'And if Trent did call the cops, there's no way they'd come – they're way too busy right now. Which also means they wouldn't have the resources to be watching him.'

'We'll still need to cut his phone line and internet,' Jack said.

'Easy.' Charlie pointed at a green box further up the road. 'I can get into that and do the job.'

'What about his mobile phone?' Obi asked.

'The panic room will see to that,' Jack said. 'Trent won't get a signal through all the steel and concrete.' He nodded at Charlie to make a start.

She jogged down the road and knelt in front of the green box. She picked the lock, opening it and exposing the wires. Charlie then waved to Jack.

'We need to move fast,' Jack said, holding up a hand and addressing Slink and Wren. 'Charlie and I will break into Trent's house. Meanwhile, you two go next door. Once Charlie's done with Trent's front door, she'll pass the lock picks to you. Got it?'

'You want us to break into the house next door?' Slink asked, looking puzzled.

'Yes. And I want you to find the nearest router or network port we can use.' Jack unzipped his bag and pulled out the coil of network cable he'd taken from the server room in the BT Tower and gave it to Slink.

Slink grinned. 'Now I get it.'

'I don't,' Wren said, frowning.

'Charlie's cutting the internet and phone to Trent's house,' Obi said. 'And Jack needs a connection to use Trent's ID to log into the Cerberus servers. We'll use the neighbour's, even if it's slow at the moment.'

'That won't matter if I'm just looking at the logs,' Jack said. 'Right, Obi, can you go round the back of the house and make sure Trent doesn't escape?'

'Sure.' Obi hurried off.

Jack looked at Charlie and lowered his hand.

She reached inside the green box, disconnected several wires, then straightened up and ran back to them.

'Let's move,' Jack said, striding across the road.

Jack and Charlie hurried up the path to Trent's house, while Slink and Wren went next door.

Charlie quickly set to work on the lock.

Jack turned his face up to the nearest CCTV camera and gave it a cold stare – hopefully Trent would be in full panic mode by now.

The lock clicked and Charlie opened the front door.

They'd been right – no alarms were activated.

She tossed the lock picks over the railing to Slink.

'You need to hurry,' Jack urged him.

'Oh, I'm all over this,' Slink said, kneeling in front of the neighbour's front door. 'Don't you worry about that.'

Jack turned back to Trent's door and took several deep breaths. 'Ready?' he asked Charlie.

'Guess so.'

Together, they entered the house and stood in the hallway.

Jack's jaw dropped.

He could not believe what he was looking at.

CHAPTER ELEVEN

JACK AND CHARLIE STOOD, ROOTED TO THE SPOT, in the hallway to Trent Myer's house. Jack was trying to get his head wrapped around what exactly he was looking at and, by the look on Charlie's face, so was she.

'Jack,' she whispered after a moment. 'Is all this what I think it is?'

He nodded. 'Yep.'

They were standing in a large room that filled at least half of the ground floor of the house.

Directly in front of them, and illuminated by spotlights, was a single chair. Only this chair was like nothing Jack had ever seen before. It had a high back and leather upholstery, and it was suspended beneath a large white frame that sat on the floor and swept behind and over it. The chair also had motors and gas struts, and looked like it could angle back for maximum comfort. Space-age mouldings and metal framework continued over the top of the chair like a futuristic scorpion's tail, and mounted on the very tip were three large screens.

It was an advanced computer station and must have cost thousands of pounds.

Jack glanced at Charlie. 'Have you ever seen anything like that before?'

'No. Obi will freak out if he sees it,' she said.

Charlie was right – it made Obi's modified dentist's chair look like a piece of junk. Mind you, Obi would be in the market for an upgraded chair after his was destroyed along with the rest of the Outlaws' bunker.

'You're positive that Trent will have run off to his panic room?' Charlie asked in a low voice.

'I think so,' Jack said. 'But we'll be careful, OK?'

'Aren't we always?'

Jack cracked a smile.

On the other side of the chair were over a hundred glass shelves mounted to the wall, and on each shelf was a different gaming console.

'Is that...?'

'Yeah,' Charlie said. 'Looks like it. Every console ever made.'

She turned back, found the light switch and flicked it on. More spotlights recessed into the ceiling came to life.

Now Jack could see more clearly, he realised that what at first glance he had thought was some weird, multicoloured wallpaper was in fact wall-to-ceiling shelves that were crammed full of old computer games boxes. Jack guessed that Trent's hard drive was stuffed with newer ones.

He looked slowly around the rest of the giant room, checking for any security cameras, but he couldn't spot any. They were either extremely well hidden or there weren't any – he couldn't be sure either way. Apart from all the shelves filled with games and consoles, the only other feature was an archway leading to a corridor.

Jack signalled to Charlie and they stepped further into the room, their eyes feasting on the impressive games library.

Charlie carefully slid a cartridge off one of the shelves and examined it, then put it back, shaking her head. 'Looks like he's got every game ever invented.'

Jack nodded. He had to agree – there were many thousands.

He walked over to the futuristic chair. Mounted to the side of it was a computer, with several lights blinking.

Jack looked at Charlie. 'Any sign of trouble, you leg it,' he said. 'Right?'

'I'm not leaving you.'

'I'm serious, Charlie.' Jack glanced at the open front door then back at her. 'If anything happens, you run. OK?'

Charlie shrugged. 'Whatever. Just get on with it, will ya?'

Jack took a breath and climbed into the chair.

As soon as he sat down, motors whirred and the chair tipped slowly backwards, the screens moved nearer and turned on, and a narrow table swung in front of him with a trackpad and keyboard fixed to it.

Jack flexed his fingers and set to work.

Charlie walked over to him as he brought up the main operating system.

'What's up with this place?' a voice said.

Jack turned to see Slink standing by the door, looking somewhere between astonished and confused. Then realisation swept across his face and he waved a finger at the walls.

'Are those all games?' he asked.

Wren joined him with an equally surprised look. 'This is amazing. I could die quite happy in here.'

'Careful what you wish for,' Jack said, glancing around the room again and feeling uneasy.

'What's that?' Slink said, gesturing to the chair. 'Some kind of space ship?'

Wren held up the end of the network cable. 'You wanted this?'

Jack nodded. 'Please.'

She hurried over and handed Jack the end of the cable.

'Can you two try to find Trent's panic room?' Jack asked them.

'No problem,' Slink said. 'Why?'

'I don't want any nasty surprises,' Jack said. 'When you find it, stand guard. Charlie and I will come looking for you once we're done here. Oh, and just stick close together, all right?'

Slink and Wren both nodded and strode from the room, through the other door and down the hallway.

Charlie took the end of the network cable from Jack and plugged it into the back of Trent's computer.

A few clicks later, Jack had a clean internet connection and was navigating to the Cerberus forum.

As he'd hoped, Trent had a moderator's login page, with his username already filled in – TYPHON. The only problem was, the password box was blank.

Charlie leant against the chair and sighed. 'Any ideas?'

Jack stared at the password box. 'No,' he muttered. 'Trent's using a customised operating system though.'

'Which means what exactly?'

'Which means,' Jack said, thinking it through, 'he has all sorts of proxies, firewalls and security programs in place to protect himself from external hackers, but hardly anything local.'

Charlie frowned. 'So is the password going to be a problem or not?'

Jack minimised the Cerberus login screen and scanned through all of Trent's installed programs. After a minute, he couldn't help but smile.

'Bingo,' Jack said. 'Trent has a program called Sitar.'

'What's that?' Charlie asked.

'A password hacker.'

Charlie laughed. 'Seriously?' she said. 'You're going to use his own program against him?'

'Yep.' Jack brought up the Cerberus forum moderator page again and set the password hacker going.

He sat back. 'This might take a while.'

'How long?' Charlie asked, glancing around.

Jack watched the letters and numbers scrolling down the screen. 'Not sure.' He turned to her. 'Wanna go check out the rest of this place?'

'Nah, not really.' She looked exhausted.

Jack forced a smile. 'Come on. Let's see if Slink and Wren have found where Trent's hiding.'

Jack slipped off the chair and walked from the room with Charlie.

Halfway down the hall, Jack stopped.

Charlie turned back. 'What's wrong?'

Jack looked left and right slowly. He had a strange feeling he was being watched.

'Jack?' Charlie whispered, stepping back to him. 'What is it?'

'It's too easy,' Jack breathed.

Charlie blinked. 'What do you mean?'

Jack moved close to her and leant into her ear. 'This is the guy that runs Cerberus, right?'

'Right.'

'The most secure website in the world,' Jack continued. 'And we just waltz right in here and start hacking his computer.'

Charlie stared at him. 'Oh no.'

Jack straightened up. 'If he let us in –'

'He's not gonna let us out,' Charlie finished.

'Let's find the others.' Jack hurried down the hallway. 'Quickly.'

The next door stood open and they peered around the corner.

A large dining table stood in the centre of the room with twelve high-backed chairs.

On the opposite wall was a marble fireplace with a portrait of a man in a suit above it. Jack assumed the man was Trent – he had blond, side-parted hair, an oval face and dark brown eyes.

Jack backed away and moved to the door at the end of the hallway. Beyond was a kitchen, modern and clean.

Jack turned to his left, looked up a flight of stairs and glanced at Charlie. 'Wait here.'

'Not a chance,' she said.

'Please, Charlie,' Jack said. 'Keep an eye on Trent's computer and let me know the moment the password is cracked. Let's get what we need and get out of here as quickly as possible.'

Charlie hesitated, then said, 'Fine. But you be careful, OK?'

Jack nodded, took a deep breath and crept up the stairs.

On the landing, he was greeted with white walls, a few modern paintings and several more doors.

The first one stood open, so Jack stepped inside.

'Slink?' he hissed. 'Wren? Where are you?'

No one answered.

The room was lined with bookshelves and cabinets filled with DVDs and Blu-rays. Another entertainment library for Trent's personal amusement. He obviously spent a lot of time at home.

A shout made Jack jump and he spun around.

'Wren?' He ran across the landing, threw open another door and went inside.

It was a bedroom with a four-poster bed and thick curtains covering the windows.

Jack's eyes darted around the room, but he couldn't see Slink or Wren anywhere.

There was a loud bang, and a few moments later Charlie came running up the stairs.

'What's wrong?' Jack asked her.

'You remember that shutter you made come down over the doors at the Millbarn building?' Charlie said, breathless. 'Well, Trent has them too – over all the windows and doors. We're trapped in here.'

Jack groaned.

'That's not all,' Charlie continued. 'The password hacker stopped and the computer turned itself off.'

'What?' Jack said, aghast.

That meant that Trent had seen what they were doing and shut it down remotely.

'Jack,' Wren shouted. 'Charlie?'

They sprinted down the hallway and stopped outside another door.

Jack put a finger to his lips, slowly turned the handle and peered inside.

This room was filled with old-fashioned arcade-game machines. All of them were on, and lights and screens flashed for attention.

Wren was kneeling on the floor in front of a kung-fu arcade-game unit. She leant over a hole in the floor with a look of panic on her face.

Jack and Charlie rushed over to her.

'What happened?' Charlie said, squatting down next to Wren and putting an arm around her shoulders.

Wren pointed a shaking finger into the hole.

With trepidation, Jack knelt and looked inside.

Below, a smooth-sided shaft dropped several metres and ended in a metal box.

Slink peered up at them with a sheepish expression.

'Yeah, all right,' he coughed. 'No need to say it.'

Jack's eyes scanned the trapdoor and that was when he noticed the electronic lock. Trent must have activated it remotely when Slink was standing directly over it, which meant – Jack glanced around the room again – there were definitely cameras in here somewhere, and probably more trapdoors too.

He straightened up. 'Charlie, please rip the curtains down from the bedroom and bring them here. We'll use them to haul Slink back up.'

Suddenly, Wren gasped as the trapdoor sprang closed, sealing Slink inside. Trent must have been listening to their conversation with hidden microphones.

'On second thoughts,' Jack said, 'no one move.'

He scanned the room for a third time. If Trent had fitted a trapdoor in here, that meant he was protecting something.

Jack closed his eyes a moment, remembering all the other rooms and the layout of the house. He imagined walking into the front room downstairs, then the dining room and kitchen. He recalled the size and the position of each, and then he worked his way up the stairs and through the movie library, the bedroom, and finally this home games arcade.

Jack opened his eyes again.

'The layout of the house,' he whispered, 'means that ...'

He leant forward, careful not to step on the trap-door, grabbed each side of the kung-fu cabinet and shoved. It swung out of the way on a pivot, revealing a spiral staircase leading down.

'No, Jack,' Charlie hissed. 'Don't do it.'

'I have to,' Jack said. 'You two stay here.'

With his heart hammering in his chest, Jack crept down the stairs.

When he reached the bottom, he was confronted with a narrow passageway with a steel door at the far end.

To the right of the door was an electronic lock, and above it was the first security camera he'd seen so far. Jack stepped in front of it and waved.

'I know you're in there.' He looked around to make sure there were no more booby traps, then faced the camera again. 'Hector's had London evacuated so he's free to steal anything he likes.' Jack coughed. 'You have to let us log into your administrator account on Cerberus so we can find him. That's why we're here. Not for you. Just Hector. You have to help us.'

A low voice came from a hidden speaker: 'I saw you on the news. You're killers.'

'No, we're not,' Jack said. 'We're trying to stop all this.'

'You're infected,' Trent snarled.

Jack sighed. 'Yeah, we are. And we're also trying to get to Hector and find the antidote.'

'There isn't a cure.'

'There is,' Jack insisted. 'And that's why we're here. You have to believe me. We're trying to stop Hector and we need to get into the Cerberus logs.'

There was a short pause, then Trent said, 'I won't let that happen. You will die here. You're not going to run free and infect anyone else.'

Jack stared up at the camera, thought about what Trent had just said and decided to try the truth.

'No one else is going to die,' Jack said. 'We're the only ones with the virus and it isn't infectious.'

This was met with silence.

Jack pressed on. 'Hector has tricked everyone. He's used us. The virus was only infectious for a short time after I was exposed to it. Even our friends that we saw soon after haven't got it.'

Still Trent didn't respond.

'Have you spoken to Hector?' Jack asked.

'Who?'

Jack was taken aback by this response. 'Hector,' he said. 'You know, the guy that's caused all this.'

There was another pause, then Trent said, 'I don't know anyone called Hector.'

'He's a member of the Cerberus forum. Quentin Del Sarto?'

'There are thousands of members of Cerberus,' Trent snapped. 'I can't be expected to remember them all.'

Jack stared back up at the camera. 'You say you know who I am, yeah?'

'Yes.'

'But you only know the propaganda,' Jack said, still thinking it through carefully. 'The lies that Hector gave to the government and the news channels.'

There was no response to this.

Jack took a deep breath. 'Look, there's a guy called Hector who tricked us. It's true – we are infected with a virus – but it's because of him. We're just trying to find Hector, get the antidote, cure ourselves and prove he's lying. That's all. Why else do you think we'd be here?'

Trent still didn't respond.

'Please,' Jack said. 'If you don't believe me, look at our Cerberus account – it'll show you some of the missions we've done and prove we're not the bad guys here.' Jack leant against the wall as a wave of dizziness washed over him and he wiped sweat from his brow. 'Just look, I'm begging you. Will you at least do that?'

He waited a full thirty seconds, but Trent didn't respond.

It's no use, Jack thought. *We're trapped.*

He looked up at the camera one last time, then sighed, turned away and ascended the spiral staircase.

As he stepped back into the room, Charlie and Wren were waiting for him, looking expectant.

Jack shook his head. 'Sorry.'

He was about to leave the room to look for something to break open the trapdoor with, when Wren gasped.

Jack looked down in shock to see the trapdoor open and Slink emerge, lifted by the floor rising from below.

Slink stepped from the hole and dusted himself off. 'Thanks, Jack.'

Jack stared at him. 'I didn't do anything.' He hesitated a moment, glanced around the room, then strode to the door before Trent changed his mind. 'Come on, guys.'

They hurried down the stairs and into the main front room.

'What happened?' Charlie said, looking between Jack and the computer that was now turned back on.

An administrator page for the Cerberus forum was open and a cursor navigated through several files. A page appeared.

Jack leant in towards the screen. 'It's the server's connection logs.' He watched as Trent scrolled down the page and highlighted Hector's IP address. 'Yes,' he said, unable to contain his excitement.

Charlie pulled the phone Noble had given them from her pocket and handed it to Jack.

He quickly brought up the internet and traced the IP address.

A map of London appeared and the image zoomed in on the IP's location.

'That can't be right,' Charlie said, looking over his shoulder at the display.

'It has to be,' Jack muttered. He held the phone up so Slink and Wren could see.

'Wait,' Wren said. 'You're saying that's where Hector's hiding?'

'Makes sense to me,' Slink said, leaning against the chair's frame. 'Kinda obvious now, really, isn't it? Come to think of it, we should have checked there first.'

Jack chuckled and nodded. Slink was right – because, now they knew, it was obvious that Hector and his father would choose such a place as their hideout.

Where was the finest accommodation in the whole of London? And where was the best security? Not to mention the fact that even if the army knew where the Del Sartos were, there was absolutely no way they'd bomb the place.

Yep, Jack thought. *It's obvious.*

'OK,' he said, standing. 'Now we know, let's get out of here.'

As they walked across the room, the steel shutter lifted from the door and Charlie, Slink and Wren left the house.

Jack turned back a moment and glanced around. 'Thank you,' he said sincerely.

Now they had real hope of getting to Hector and the antidote.

CHAPTER TWELVE

JACK, CHARLIE, SLINK AND WREN WALKED DOWN the road, away from Trent Myer's house.

Obi joined them. 'Did you find out Hector's location?' he asked in a hoarse voice.

'Yep,' Slink replied. 'Buckingham Palace.'

Obi snorted. 'No, really, where is he?'

'That's where he really is,' Jack said. He looked at Charlie as they rounded a corner and continued walking. 'So, let me think this through a minute. We need blueprints of Buckingham Palace, which we don't have, and we need gadgets to break in, which we don't have either.'

Charlie pulled her jacket collar up and shivered. 'Yeah, that's about the size of it.'

'OK,' Jack said. 'I can't do anything about the plans, but I have an idea where we can find a ton of supplies for you to build some awesome gadgets.' He forced a grin at her.

Charlie's eyebrows lifted. 'Oh yeah? Where's that then? We're not gonna break into an electrical shop, are we?'

'No,' Jack said, increasing his stride the best he could. 'But what's the one place in London that has everything we need, and where we don't technically have to steal a thing?'

Charlie glanced back at Obi and the other Outlaws and shrugged. 'As long as it's somewhere warm, I don't care.'

'Come on,' Jack said. 'I'll show you.'

The five Outlaws stood across the road from Baker Street Underground station.

There was a steel grille door covering the entrance.

Jack looked left and right. All the buildings were in darkness and only the street lamps were on. It was late at night and, for once, there were no other sounds – no sirens or alarms, no shouts.

Jack wondered if the army had rounded up as many people as they could and had now left London. Or maybe the remaining Londoners were too frightened to leave their homes.

Jack was also curious as to how long the power would stay on. With no employees manning the power stations, there was no one to control them. How long could they run on their own? Without power, the Outlaws' next task would be near impossible.

'I hate to break it to ya, Jack,' Slink said, gesturing across the road at Baker Street station's entrance, 'but I'm pretty sure the trains aren't running at the moment.'

Jack nodded and leant against a lamp post. 'You could be right.' He coughed and rubbed his chest. 'But the station isn't our target.' He pointed two doors down. '*That* is.'

All eyes moved to where Jack indicated, and he watched as smiles spread across each of their faces.

Charlie nudged Jack's arm. 'That's really clever.'

'I know,' Jack said.

Charlie rolled her eyes. 'Nice to see Captain Modest is still with us.'

Obi sneezed, making them all jump. 'Sorry.'

'Wait a minute,' Wren said. 'We're going to break into the lost property office? How? We don't have tools.'

She was right – it too was secured with steel shutters.

'We'll get in.' Jack turned to Charlie and handed her Abdul's phone. 'Call Raze, please, and have him bring the others here urgently. Tell them to load up food and as many supplies as they can carry from the cavern.'

'Sure.' Charlie turned away and pressed the phone to her ear.

Next, Jack looked at Obi, Slink and Wren. Under the artificial street lighting, they seemed paler than ever and their eyes had sunk into their heads. There was no doubt about it – they were looking more and more like zombies. If Jack didn't hurry up and get this mission sorted out soon, none of them would be strong enough to continue.

'Raze, Domino, Ryan and Wilf are on their way,' Charlie said, hanging up and returning to the group.

'Good. Come on.'

The five Outlaws hurried down the road and stopped outside a wrought-iron gate sandwiched between two buildings.

Slink slapped his hands together. 'Easy peasy lemon squeezy.' He leapt up, grabbed the top of the gate and froze.

'What's wrong?' Jack asked.

'Can't. Do. It,' Slink grunted. 'No strength left.' He turned his head to look at them. 'Help me then.'

Jack and Charlie rushed forward, took Slink's legs and pushed him up and over the top of the gate.

Once on the other side, Slink hit the ground hard and staggered backwards, almost losing his balance.

Jack cringed. This wasn't a good sign.

Slink swore, straightened up and blew out a puff of air. 'Stupid virus,' he grumbled.

He unbolted the gate and let the others through.

They made their way down the narrow walkway and came out at the back of the buildings. Straight in front of them were several stationary trains on the tracks.

It seemed so strange to Jack to see them there, quiet, like metal corpses – he was used to the Underground running practically all night and day. With everywhere silent and still, it didn't feel like London at all.

The Outlaws kept to the right-hand side of the tracks and stopped outside the rear exit of the lost property office.

Charlie examined the door, but there was no handle or lock. 'There's no simple way to get through this.'

'We don't need to go that way,' Jack said, pointing at a small window at their feet. 'That's the basement. That's our target.'

'Way ahead of you.' Slink had a metal pole in his hands.

'Where did you get that?' Wren asked.

Slink indicated a pile of scrap metal, broken pallets and rubbish over his shoulder. And, before anyone could stop him, he thrust the pole at the window, punching a hole straight through the glass.

Slink then pulled back and rammed the pole forward again, enlarging the hole until it was ten centimetres in diameter. Then he knelt down, reached through and undid the clasp on the inside.

Slink straightened up, threw the pole away and stared at the window. 'Well, I only know of one person who can fit through that gap.'

They all turned to Wren.

She frowned and peered through the window opening. 'It's dark in there.'

'Since when have you ever been scared of anything?' Obi said.

'Here you are.' Jack handed her Charlie's pocket torch.

She swallowed. 'Fine.'

Obi and Slink took an arm each and helped Wren sit down, then she swung her legs inside and wriggled through the window.

Obi called after her, 'You all right in there?'

'Yeah, I'm OK.' Wren flicked the torch on and shone it around the room.

'The back door's probably in a corridor,' Jack said. 'Somewhere to your right.'

'I'll find it,' Wren grumbled. She banged into a table. 'Ow,' she muttered under her breath as she disappeared from view.

A minute later, and much to everyone's relief, the back door opened and Wren stuck her head out.

'This place is really weird, I hope you know that.'

Jack ushered everyone through.

Once they were safely inside, he shut the door, found a light switch and flicked it on.

They were now standing in a hallway with white walls that reminded Jack of an old-fashioned hospital. Down the left-hand side stood several steel cages on wheels.

For a second, Jack imagined locking Hector in one of them and shoving him down a very steep hill. He shook himself back to reality, but wouldn't completely dismiss the idea if the opportunity arose.

Ahead was a set of double doors. They stepped through them and into a large room with shelves and racks crammed full of objects.

There was everything from wallets, keys, purses, handbags, glasses, school bags and suitcases, to buggies, mobile phones, tablets, laptops and trainers. There was even a grandfather clock and next to it was a bucket filled with false teeth.

The five Outlaws stared at it all.

'Treasure,' Wren breathed.

'Look at this place,' Obi said, his eyes bulging. 'There must be hundreds of thousands of things in here.'

'Yeah,' Jack said. 'All the stuff people lose on trains and buses around London.' He strode between the shelves, trying to take it all in.

There were road signs, toys, a knight's helmet, clocks, watches, samurai swords, gas masks, backpacks and even several radio-controlled cars complete with transmitters. Every item had a paper tag fixed to it with an identification number, description and a location.

Jack returned to Charlie. 'So, what do you think?'

'What do you mean?'

'Would you feel bad using some of this stuff to make your gadgets?'

Charlie shook her head. 'Nope.'

'Good.' Jack walked from the storeroom and the others followed him into a sorting office packed with desks and long grey benches. In the corner of the room was a metal spiral chute that led from the floor above.

'Bagsy I get a go on the slide first,' Slink said.

'I don't think it's safe for people,' Obi said. 'They must send lost stuff down it from upstairs.'

'Hmm.' Slink scratched his chin. 'We'll test it out with Wren first then.'

She gave him a playful punch on the arm.

'Ouch.' Slink rubbed his arm. 'Careful, I'm feeling delicate.'

'We all are.' Jack dropped into a seat in front of a monitor and switched on the computer. He checked it over. 'There's no internet here, but they do have every single item catalogued, which is going to be handy.'

Abdul's phone beeped and Charlie looked at the display. 'The others are here.'

She strode from the room and returned a few moments later with Raze, Domino, Wilf and Ryan. They each carried backpacks full to bursting.

'This place is cool,' Ryan said, unzipping his bag and pulling out crisps, bread, cheese and biscuits.

Raze, Wilf and Domino did the same, and when they were done, they had a mountain of food and drink in front of them.

Raze handed everyone cans of lemonade and looked about. 'Is this your new base then?'

'For the time being,' Jack said. He nodded at the supplies. 'Thanks for bringing all this.'

'Any time.' Domino grinned, but the smile slipped from her face as she noticed the Outlaws' haggard faces.

As everyone tucked in, Jack grabbed a pen and notepad and started writing. When he was done, he showed it to Charlie. 'Here's a list of gadgets I think we're going to need for this mission.'

She took it from him and her eyebrows knitted together as she read. 'Jack, I don't see how any of this will help us break in, or even what we want to break in for. Hector's not just going to hand the antidote over and stand aside.'

'You remember Noble gave me that?' Jack nodded at Abdul's phone. 'Said that he'd put his own phone number in the contacts list?'

Charlie cleared her throat. 'Yeah?'

'Well, I think he not only sacrificed himself to draw those cops away from us, but he wanted to get caught.'

'Why?' Charlie said. 'Why would Noble do that?'

'Think about it. Noble is now with the cops or the army or whoever. Right?'

She nodded.

'I think he wants us to get a confession out of Hector,' Jack said.

Charlie stared a moment, then her eyes widened, as she seemed to understand. She gestured to the phone. 'You're saying we need to have that on us, with a call in progress to Noble, and get Hector to spill his guts?'

'Yep.'

'Oh. That should be easy then,' Charlie said in a sarcastic tone. She looked at the list again. 'I hope you've got a good plan, Jack. I really could do with a bit of a lie-down when this is all over.'

'I hope so too.' Jack gritted his teeth. He was determined to bring Hector and his father down. No messing about this time – this was where it ended, one way or another.

'A cylinder on a miniature parachute and an oxygen tank fixed inside a car...' Charlie looked up at him. 'How are they going to help us break into Buckingham Palace? Won't it have some serious security?'

Jack smiled. 'I'll explain it properly later, but it's going to involve you doing some expert driving. Hector will have taken care of the security at the palace already. What we're going to have problems with is –'

'His hired goons,' Charlie finished.

'Exactly right. They'll be armed and we'll be pretty much the only thing in London that's moving.' Jack offered her a weak smile. 'So,' he said, nodding at the list. 'How long d'you think it'll take you to build all of that?'

Charlie pursed her lips a moment then said, 'If everyone helps me, I dunno, twelve hours, maybe less?'

'Can we aim for less, please?' Jack asked with half a forced smile. He wasn't sure if any of them had much time left in them.

Charlie sighed. 'I'll do my best.'

'You always do.' Jack faced the computer and cracked his knuckles. 'Let's get started.'

Charlie sketched designs for the gadgets and once she'd worked out what items she needed to make them, Jack searched the lost property database. When he had an item's location, he jotted it down on a piece of paper and handed it to one of the others, who hunted it down.

Pretty soon they were all working well together.

'This looks good,' Charlie said, eyeing a Bluetooth headset Ryan had just handed to her. 'We'll need to find a charger for it.'

Jack scanned the list. 'Try this,' he said, writing down a number and passing it to Ryan.

Ryan jogged off and was replaced by Wren. She gave Charlie a pair of lenses encased in brass with a handle to one side.

Charlie frowned at them. 'Er, why do I need these?'

Wren held up the piece of paper Jack had given her. 'Mini binoculars. Although they weren't where you said they were, Jack.'

Slink laughed.

Wren whirled around to face him and put her hands on her hips. 'What?'

'Those aren't binoculars, you bozo,' Slink said with a raspy laugh. 'They're opera glasses.'

'Keep laughing at her,' Charlie warned him, 'and when we get out of this mess, I'll take you to the ballet.'

Slink fell instantly silent. 'I'm not watching people prance about in tights.' He turned in a circle. 'Oh, la-di-da.'

Charlie rolled her eyes.

'Wait a minute, Slink,' Jack said. 'You watch those superhero movies and pretty much all those guys wear tights.'

Slink's face dropped and now it was Wren who was laughing.

Jack handed her another piece of paper. 'Try this location instead,' he said. 'And grab us two pairs, please.'

Wren took the paper from him, poked her tongue out at Slink and scurried off.

Slink, Raze and Wilf handed Charlie several backpacks each.

'These look perfect,' she said, setting them on the floor by her feet.

Jack passed the last piece of paper to Raze. 'Mobile phones.'

'We need ones with plenty of charge left in the battery,' Charlie added.

'On it.' Raze hurried off.

Charlie glanced around. She now had a mountain of stuff all around her and she consulted her drawings. 'I think this should pretty much do it, Jack.'

Jack stood and stretched. 'Great. I need to do a recon mission of Buckingham Palace. Slink, can you come with me?'

'No worries.'

They left the room and as they strode down the corridor, Wren reappeared with two pairs of binoculars.

Jack took them from her. 'Thanks.'

'Where are you going?' she asked.

'Recon mission. Please help Charlie build those gadgets. We shouldn't be too long.'

'Be careful,' Wren said.

'Aren't we always?' Slink said as they walked towards the exit.

'No, actually. You're never careful.'

Thirty minutes later, Jack and Slink were standing down the road from Buckingham Palace.

Jack held Slink back. 'Don't get too close,' he warned. 'We don't want them seeing us.'

They stepped to the trunk of the nearest tree, peered round and raised the binoculars to their eyes.

'Are you seeing what I'm seeing, Jack?'

'Yeah.'

On the roof of the palace were several armed men. Three were walking slowly around the edge, with automatic weapons slung over their shoulders, while two men were lying down holding sniper rifles.

255

'What d'you reckon the range is on those?' Slink asked.

'Put it this way,' Jack said. 'We're close enough to get shot.'

They glanced at each other and slowly backed away.

Slink and Jack were careful to stay out of sight of the snipers as they circled around the palace, peering between buildings. Every now and again, vans and lorries would come and go.

'You reckon Hector's looting the place?' Slink asked.

Jack watched one van head in the direction of the Thames and nodded. His bet was on Hector loading up a ship somewhere nearby – that was the only way he could escape London. Knowing Hector, he would've made sure there was an escape plan in place, especially as he'd gone to all this trouble.

The Outlaws needed to move fast. Who knew when Hector and his father planned to leave?

Jack looked back at Buckingham Palace.

Hector's men were focused mainly on the front of the building, where they obviously thought they were most vulnerable.

That left the palace gardens. The only problem was, the grounds were surrounded by a ten-foot-high brick wall topped with metal spikes, razor wire and barbed wire for another few feet beyond that.

As they stood across the road from the back of the palace in Grosvenor Place, Jack's imagination clicked into high gear. He thought of a giant catapult flinging the Urban Outlaws over the wall, one by one, to land safely on the palace lawn.

Yeah, right, he thought.

'Jack,' Slink hissed, nudging him.

'What?'

Slink pointed at several cameras mounted on a pole on the other side of the wall. Because of the trees behind them, they hadn't been so easy to spot.

Jack nodded. 'Bit of a problem.'

Slink looked at him. 'You've got this though, right?'

Jack sighed. 'I hope so.'

CHAPTER THIRTEEN

BY THE TIME JACK AND SLINK RETURNED TO Baker Street's lost property office, Charlie and the others were stuck into the gadget-building operation.

Charlie had the back of a mobile phone open and was using a soldering iron to modify components, while Obi, Wren and Ryan were cutting and sewing bits of fabric. Raze, Wilf and Domino were also busy, stripping lengths of wire and fixing connectors to the ends.

Jack couldn't help but smile. 'Now this is teamwork, Charlie.'

'If we ever get out of all this mess,' Charlie said, sniffing, 'I might just use these guys for everything I make from now on. I'd get things done ten times quicker.'

Wren held up her hands. Several fingers on each had plasters. 'I don't think I'm too great at sewing though.'

'I'll go get a blowtorch,' Slink said. 'Maybe you'll be better at metalworking.'

'No.' Charlie glanced up. 'Let's keep Wren's activities to ones that don't involve flammable materials.'

Wren coughed. 'What are you trying to say?'

Charlie gestured to the chair next to her. 'Sit here, Slink. Now you're back, you can help me with this.'

'Where's Abdul's phone?' Jack asked.

Charlie pointed to a bench across the room. 'Charging.'

Jack went over to the socket, unplugged the phone and left the room with it.

He walked down the corridor, found a small office and sat behind the desk.

Jack rubbed his eyes. He felt dizzy for a moment and had the urge to never get up again. He knew that pretty soon the virus would stop him altogether.

Just a few more hours, he thought. In a few hours, it would be over and he could sleep all he wanted.

Jack blinked a few times, trying to clear his grogginess, and focused on the phone's display. The signal was weak, but he managed to get an internet connection, and after a minute or two of surfing, he found a basic plan for Buckingham Palace. As he'd expected, there were no detailed blueprints, but he didn't need them – all he wanted was a rough outline of the room locations.

Jack stared at the plan, wondering which of those rooms Hector was likely to be in. There was no way to tell where he was – or where he was storing the antidote.

Jack also wondered if Hector would try to destroy the antidote if the Outlaws got too close. He doubted it though, because without the antidote Hector had no leverage over the government, nothing to blackmail them with. At the moment, he was likely to be dangling it in front of their faces like a carrot – 'Get everyone out of London and I *might* let you have it.'

Jack also imagined that the reason why the government hadn't tried to raid Hector and take the antidote – besides Hector's high-profile and valuable hiding place – was the possibility that they might cause Hector to destroy the antidote.

If only they knew they didn't need the antidote at all, that would change the balance of power. But that needed proof.

Jack examined the plan of Buckingham Palace and pictured the snipers and armed guards patrolling the grounds. Most of Hector's men were focused on protecting the front of the building, which left the rear of the premises their only chance.

The Outlaws would need to get over the wall, run through the grounds – keeping clear of any guards – then find the nearest door and pick the lock. And that's when a new idea struck him, but before Jack had time to think it through properly, Charlie entered the room.

'Are you OK?' she said.

He nodded. 'Yeah.' Jack set the phone down. 'You? How are the gadgets coming along?'

'The gadgets are looking good,' she said. 'I'm not sure about the whole thing with the car though.'

'Can't you get one?' Jack asked.

'That's not the problem,' Charlie said. 'There's a car that's perfect for the job back at my dad's garage.'

'So what's the problem?'

'You need to tell me the whole plan.'

Jack nodded. 'I do. You're right.'

He then proceeded to tell her, explaining what the car was for and what he needed her to do.

When he'd finished, Charlie's eyebrows rose. 'Are you serious? That's really dangerous, Jack.'

'Look,' Jack said in a soft voice. 'You don't have to do it. I won't make you.'

'You never make us do anything,' Charlie said. 'We follow your plans because we want to.' She smiled and it lit up her tired face. 'And because none of us could come up with anything close to your ideas.'

'Of course you could,' Jack said. 'Just try the first crazy thing that pops into your head. That's pretty much what I do.' He coughed and winced – his lungs felt like they were about to collapse.

Charlie leant against the wall. 'I'm exhausted.'

Jack sat back in the chair. 'We all are. We should be in a hospital, not running around after an egotistical kid and his equally crazy father.'

Charlie half-smiled back at him. 'At least we're all ill,' she said. 'Outlaws go through everything together – as always, right?'

'Right.' Although Jack wished it was just him that was infected.

Charlie seemed to notice his anxiety. 'This mission won't fail, will it?'

Jack shook his head, even though he was never confident about missions and this one was definitely no exception. But the truth was that failure literally wasn't an option on this mission. If they failed, they died. That simple. However, if they didn't at least try, they'd be dead pretty soon anyway.

'How much longer do you want to get everything done?' he asked.

Charlie glanced at the list. 'I'd say about another couple of hours.'

'Really?' Jack said. 'That's great.'

'Like I told ya – we've got an amazing team.'

'Yes, we do.'

Charlie walked to the door.

'Charlie?'

She turned back.

'Thank you,' Jack said.

'For what?'

'For everything. You know, for being my friend.'

Charlie stared at him. 'You make it sound like we're not coming back.'

Jack didn't respond to that because he had no words left to describe how he was feeling right at that moment.

Charlie seemed to understand. 'It'll all be OK, Jack. You'll see.' She went to leave, but hesitated. 'I think I can guess what most of these items are for now, but I've been meaning to ask you – that cata- pult? What's the deal there?'

'That's purely for Hector's benefit,' Jack said.

Charlie nodded. 'Plan B. I always hate Plan B.' She winked and left.

Jack sat in silence for a minute, staring at the door, remembering all the good times with Charlie and the other Outlaws. Then he shook himself back to the present moment, and started to run through the plan again, improving and refining it. It would be all on him – he couldn't mess any part of this up, otherwise his friends would die.

True to her word – a couple of hours later, Charlie reappeared.

'I think we're ready,' she said.

Jack stood, followed her into the sorting room and looked around at them all.

Raze, Wilf, Ryan and Domino seemed excited. But Charlie, Obi, Slink and Wren looked paler and more exhausted than ever.

Jack took a deep breath. 'I could give you this big speech about how this is going to be the toughest mission of our lives, and how important it is that we don't fail, but you already know that.' He paced back and forth. 'You also know that Hector and his father need to be brought down once and for all. We can't let them continue. It has to end.' Jack looked between them all. 'You already know that we need to find the antidote too.' He took a deep, juddering breath and let it out slowly. 'But what I don't tell you enough is how much you guys mean to me. God only knows where I'd be – or who I'd be – without you lot. I love you all. You're my family.'

Wren ran over to Jack and threw her arms around his waist. 'I love you too, Jack,' she whispered.

Charlie and Obi joined in the hug.

Jack looked over at Slink and was surprised to see tears in his eyes.

'What?' Slink said. 'I'm not crying.' He sniffed and wiped them with his sleeve. 'It's the bug.'

Obi frowned at him. 'Get over here, you idiot.'

'You lot are always so sentimental.' Slink hesitated a moment longer, then joined them for a group hug.

Jack closed his eyes and hoped his friends would get to see better days ahead.

Jack, Obi, Slink and Wren stood in Grosvenor Place, facing the rear wall that bordered Buckingham Palace.

'How are we all going to get over that?' Obi asked.

'Not all of us need to. Right,' Jack said, looking at them all in turn. 'Let's do this. But, please, everyone be careful and follow the plan exactly, OK?'

They all gave a solemn nod and it was apparent that they were thinking the same thing he was – the mission was likely to fail. They were all so weak. They hardly had enough strength to stand upright, let alone carry out such an important mission.

Jack's stomach knotted as he thought about what was to come. He had run through the plan so many times in his head, but there was no way to eliminate the danger.

Slink's forlorn expression softened as he seemed to notice Jack's anxiety. 'Your plans are always completely crazy and dangerous – what's so different now?'

'The difference is that we have a virus and we're not at our best,' Jack said, voicing his fears.

'Even your off days are way better than most people's best ones,' Obi said. 'I know your plan will work, crazy or not.'

'Thanks.' Jack frowned. 'I think.' He turned back to face the wall. 'Come on then, let's get it over with.'

They walked across the road and Jack checked the coast was clear again. London was lifeless and empty. Throughout its entire history, even during the World Wars, Jack doubted it had ever been so quiet.

'We're ready,' he said into his headset.

They watched as a car rounded the corner then mounted the kerb, close to the wall, and stopped in front of them.

Charlie waved from behind the wheel.

It was the only car left in her dad's garage that still worked, but it was perfect for the job – an old jeep with a high roof.

With a lot of effort, Jack and Slink climbed on to the bonnet then on to the roof of the car. Their heads barely came in line with the top of the palace wall's brickwork.

Wren opened the rear passenger door and started passing heavy blankets, duvets and yoga mats up to them. Jack and Slink placed them all over the first level of wall spikes.

When they were sure they had enough padding, Wren passed up a set of bolt cutters. She then closed the car door and watched them in silence.

Jack braced his back against the wall and made a stirrup with his hands. 'Go on then.'

Slink stepped up and straddled the blankets. 'Quite comfortable, actually. I might have a nap.'

'Don't push your luck,' Jack muttered. 'Those spikes are sharp.' He handed Slink the bolt cutters.

Slink braced his feet, stood up, then cut each wire in the fence above him.

Jack watched and listened. He wasn't sure if the fence was alarmed and was relieved that, so far, no sirens had sounded.

'Done,' Slink said, passing the bolt cutters back and nodding at a security camera on a pole directly in front of him. 'You're right – I can make that.'

'Are you sure?' Jack asked.

Slink cricked his neck and flexed his arms. 'I can do it. Just need to loosen up a bit.'

'Take your time,' Jack insisted, his chest tightening. If Slink missed, the entire mission would be over.

Slink swung his legs over the spikes and blankets, and crouched down on top of the wall. He looked around to make sure no guards had spotted him, then took several deep breaths and kept his focus on the pole that was a couple of metres away.

Jack clenched his fists. *Please don't miss. Please don't miss*, he thought. The fall would seriously injure Slink, if not worse.

Suddenly, yet as if in slow motion, Slink leapt from the top of the wall, his hands outstretched.

Jack's breath caught and his eyes went wide as he watched Slink fly through the air.

Slink hit the pole hard, and for a split second Jack thought he was going to fall, but he managed to wrap his legs around it and grab the camera mount.

Jack relaxed. 'Good work, mate.'

'Thanks.' Even Slink couldn't hide his relief at having made it.

Slink removed a screwdriver from his back pocket and, with trembling fingers, unscrewed the base of the camera.

Jack slipped off his backpack and took out the length of cable Raze, Wild and Domino had worked on. 'Here,' he said, tossing one end of it over to Slink.

Slink took a minute or two to connect the wires and check they were secure before giving Jack the thumbs-up.

Jack lowered the other end of the cable to Wren. She took it over to Obi, who was sitting on the ground cross-legged, with a laptop open in front of him.

Obi connected the wires to the laptop and after a few clicks on the trackpad he looked up at Jack. 'I'm in.'

Jack turned to Slink. 'OK. You're clear. But wait for us to tell you when to move.'

Slink nodded and slid down the pole, out of sight.

Jack climbed from the roof of the jeep and hurried over to Obi and Wren.

Obi had a screen up and he was scrolling through the palace's CCTV images. They showed various views around the grounds and he could see several guards patrolling.

'I'm recording now,' Obi said. 'Need another minute before I can loop it.'

Obi had to be careful with recording the CCTV and then looping it because anyone watching the monitors would see a jump in the images or notice the guard patrolling the same spot over and over.

Jack tensed and counted off the seconds.

It looked as though Obi had hacked into around twenty cameras, but Jack's primary concern was the six that covered the planned route Slink would take from his current location to the back of the palace.

'Any luck with inside the building?' Jack asked Obi after a couple of minutes.

Obi shook his head. 'No internal cameras,' he said. 'They must be on a separate system.'

Jack sighed, but he'd prepared for that eventuality. He couldn't lie though – it definitely would have been a bonus if he could see what was happening inside the palace. That way, he'd have known for sure where Hector and his father were, not to mention how many goons they had protecting them.

'Shall I just go?' Slink said in their headsets after another minute had passed.

Jack cupped a hand over the microphone. 'No,' he said. 'Stick to the plan.'

'But there's no one here,' Slink whispered.

'There is,' Obi said. 'Ten metres to your right.'

There was a short pause, then Slink said, 'He's walking the other way. He won't see me. I could make a run for it.'

'Please,' Jack said, 'just stick to the plan, mate.'

It was crucial they all did.

'OK. Fine,' Slink huffed. 'I'm only trying to speed this up a bit.'

'I know,' Jack said. 'And I appreciate it. But now's not the time to go rogue on us.'

Another agonising minute passed, then Obi hit a few buttons and glanced at Jack. 'They're watching looped recordings now. It's safe.' He then linked the cameras directly to the laptop so only they could see the real images.

'OK, Slink,' Jack said into his headset. 'You can move.'

Jack, Obi and Wren watched Slink step into view on one of the palace cameras, slip off his backpack and take out a radio-controlled car with its own camera mounted to the top and two antennae jutting from the side.

It wasn't as sophisticated as the drones Charlie had made before – Shadow Bee and Robbie – but she'd done a fantastic job in such a short space of time with limited resources.

Slink set the car down and stepped back.

Jack removed the radio transmitter from his own bag and handed it to Wren.

Her eyes widened. 'Me?'

'You're the best at it. Just go slow.'

Wren grinned.

She was the supreme champ at *Track 76*, the racing arcade game back at the bunker –

Jack stopped that thought before he could let the surging wave of their loss wash over him. Right now, he needed to focus.

Wren sat next to Obi as he brought up the camera view from the radio-controlled car.

Jack crouched down next to them. He brought up the plan of the palace on his phone. 'Go, Wren.'

Wren pushed forward on the joystick and the car raced off.

Obi kept his attention on the security cameras, watching out for guards, as he guided Wren through the trees, across the lawn, past hedgerows and flower beds, until she finally went up a short flight of steps, across the palace's rear terrace and stopped.

Jack looked at the time – it had taken just under four minutes.

'There,' he said, pointing at a door on the right of the screen. 'That's Slink's target.'

According to the plan on the phone, the door opened on to a dining room.

Jack pressed a finger to his ear. 'Slink, you're up, but please follow Obi's instructions to the letter. And no heroics, right?'

'You always spoil my fun,' Slink's hoarse voice replied.

Jack stood. 'See you in a while,' he said to Obi and Wren.

He watched them for a few seconds, then forced himself to turn away and stride to the four-by-four.

He clambered into the passenger seat and fastened the seat belt.

'Are you all right?' Charlie asked him.

'Yeah,' Jack said, although he felt far from all right – he wanted to get this over with as soon as possible. 'Let's go.'

Charlie waved at Obi and Wren, then pulled off the kerb and headed up the road.

She took side streets, careful to stay out of a direct line of sight from the palace.

Charlie stopped the jeep a little way down Birdcage Walk, a road that ran almost parallel to the Mall.

She looked over at Jack. 'Are you sure about this?'

'Nope.'

'Me neither.' Charlie looked forward again. 'I guess now's not a good time to ask if you have any better plans?'

Jack shook his head. 'This is all I've got.'

Charlie bit her lip. 'OK. As long as you're sure.'

'I'm never sure,' Jack muttered.

For a few moments, they stared straight ahead, then Charlie revved the engine and did a wheelspin down the road.

Jack was thrown to the side as she took a sharp right on to Spur Road and aimed the four-by-four directly at the palace.

Shots rang out and thudded into the car door.

Jack and Charlie ducked in their seats, and she pressed her foot hard to the floor.

'Brace,' Charlie screamed.

She let go of the steering wheel and crossed her arms.

An instant later, the car slammed into Buckingham Palace's gates with a sickening smash and the windscreen shattered as it was hit by a barrage of bullets.

Jack peered forward, but the gates had sustained minimal damage.

Charlie threw the car into reverse, spun it around and accelerated away, as another hail of bullets thudded all around them.

As she sped down the Mall, Charlie glanced in a side mirror. 'Here they come.'

Jack looked over his shoulder to see a black SUV in hot pursuit. 'It's Connor,' he said, turning forward.

Charlie slammed her foot down on the accelerator and shoved the gearstick into fourth.

'Let's see how good he is at driving,' she said, ripping the steering wheel hard over, first right, then left down Great Scotland Yard.

The SUV rammed them from behind. The four-by-four wobbled dangerously, but Charlie managed to regain control.

'I guess he's annoyed.'

'I think you could be right,' Jack said, as they screeched around the corner.

At the end of the road, Charlie turned left under Golden Jubilee Bridges and along the River Thames.

The SUV hit them again, harder this time.

Jack had never seen Charlie look so intense.

For a moment, the reality and danger of the situation hit him, but before he had time to really think about it, the SUV slammed into them for a third time.

The four-by-four swerved violently and Charlie fought to bring it under control. She managed it, dropped down a gear and accelerated away.

She glanced at Jack and their eyes met briefly, anxiety mirrored in their faces.

Before Jack could say anything, Charlie veered across the road and aimed for a set of steps.

'Brace!' she shouted.

A fraction of a second later, they hit the steps, smashed through a stone wall and flew into the air.

Jack closed his eyes as the car arced over the river, and he prayed they would both live through this.

CHAPTER FOURTEEN

THE CAR HIT THE WATER AND JACK WAS SLAMMED forwards and to the left, smacking his head on the passenger window.

Dazed, he fell back and felt icy cold water around his feet.

Jack looked over at Charlie.

'I'm all right,' she said, touching a cut above her left eye.

Jack grabbed the window winder and gasped as it came off in his hand.

'It's OK,' Charlie said, as water poured in around them. 'Don't panic. You can use the door but you won't be able to open it until the car is completely flooded.'

'I know,' Jack replied, remembering their discussion about the water pressure and how she'd escape later. 'You sure you'll be OK?' Now the reality of the situation was setting in and, as the icy water moved up his legs, Jack wasn't convinced this plan was the best he could have come up with.

'I'll be fine,' Charlie said, pulling down her shirt collar to reveal the homemade wetsuit beneath her clothes.

Under Charlie's supervision, Wren had made one for each of them. Although the makeshift wetsuits only protected their torsos and upper arms, Jack hoped they would do a good job at preventing their core temperatures from falling too low. The last thing they needed on top of the virus was hypothermia.

Charlie reached down by her seat and pulled out the end of a nylon tube. It was connected to a couple of empty plastic tanks she'd fitted in the boot – hopefully Charlie would have enough air for ten minutes whilst submerged.

The green water rose up the bonnet of the car, over the windscreen, and darkness enveloped them as the jeep dropped below the surface.

The water came in faster now, and as it continued up Jack's chest and touched his neck, he said, 'Charlie?'

'Yeah?'

'Please live through this.'

'I intend to.'

'Promise?'

But before she had time to answer, the water rose over their heads.

Jack held his breath and waited until all the air had been forced from the car. Then he undid his seat belt, grabbed the door handle and pushed.

It didn't open.

Jack shoved again, but the door still would not budge.

Panic immediately gripped him. Jack shouldered the door again and again, but no matter how hard he tried, it wouldn't move.

His chest started to burn.

He was going to drown.

What a stupid way to die, he thought.

And it was *his* fault. It was his dumb plan that had done it. He should've taken longer to –

Suddenly, Jack felt Charlie reach across him, yank up the lock and open the door.

Jack didn't hesitate. He pushed through, out into the river, and kicked hard for the surface.

As soon as his head broke into open air, he gasped and took big lungfuls of oxygen.

Stunned to still be alive, Jack gathered his senses and swam to the nearest set of steps. He hauled himself from the water with every last bit of strength he had, and, just as he'd predicted, a pair of hands grabbed his shoulders.

Jack wiped water from his eyes and looked up at Connor.

'Where's the other one?' he snarled, his face a centimetre from Jack's.

Jack shook his head and pretended to fight back tears. 'Gone.'

Connor's eyes narrowed and he looked at the river for a long moment, as if expecting Charlie's head to pop up at any time. But when a couple of minutes had passed, he let out an angry grunt, spun around and dragged Jack to the SUV.

He threw Jack on to the passenger seat and slid in the driver's side. He started the engine and the SUV pulled away.

Jack shivered. 'Have you got a towel?'

Connor didn't respond. He just held a gun in his lap, aimed up at Jack's chest, while he drove.

Jack looked at the gun, then his eyes lifted to Connor's. 'There's no point threatening me.' He coughed. 'I'm dead already.'

A smile tugged the corners of Connor's lips. 'I know.'

Jack hugged himself and sat back.

Connor kept his gaze forward, pressing his lips together and obviously fighting the urge to shoot him.

They wove through the streets and Jack closed his eyes.

His body felt so cold and stiff, and he ached so badly that he just wanted to die right there and then. But, as he always did, he thought of the other Outlaws – his family. He owed it to them to hold it together.

They needed him.

Just a little while longer, he thought.

Everything was in place, Jack reminded himself. Connor thought Charlie was dead, and the other Outlaws were playing their parts.

Now it was all up to him. This was it. No slip-ups from here on. It had to be perfect.

Jack gritted his teeth, opened his eyes and saw that they were driving up the Mall.

They reached the end, swept around the Queen Victoria Memorial and stopped at the gates of Buckingham Palace.

Jack leant forward and peered up at the immense building through the windscreen.

It was official, he thought. Hector and his father were one hundred per cent crazy, and the only thing that could beat crazy was someone crazier.

Today, that would have to be him.

A man, dressed in black and carrying an automatic rifle, opened the gate and the SUV drove through.

Connor slowed the car as they approached the central archway and nodded at another armed guard, who waved them on.

They headed across a gigantic inner forecourt that was surrounded on all sides by the palace building.

The whole area was a hive of activity, crammed full of trucks and vans with men loading crates, boxes and bags. It was like Talya's warehouse and gang, only scaled up a thousand times.

As they drove past, Jack watched two men load a golden throne into the back of a van.

'Where are they taking it all?' Jack asked, half-knowing the answer already.

Connor considered him a moment and then, probably realising it didn't matter what Jack knew any more, he said, 'The Thames. Hector has ships waiting.'

Connor parked the SUV behind a Rolls-Royce and next to a door with another armed man guarding it.

Connor climbed out and waved his gun, gesturing for Jack to follow.

With effort, Jack edged his way across the seat and stepped from the car.

Connor patted him down, removing a phone and headset along with several other objects from his pockets.

'With us,' he said to the guard.

Then Jack followed Connor into the palace, with the guard bringing up the rear.

The interior of the palace wasn't far from what Jack had imagined it to be, with its polished marble and wood flooring, large portraits hanging on the walls, crystal chandeliers and ornate furniture that looked like it belonged in a museum.

Almost everything was accented in gold leaf.

More men were wrapping it all up, ready to move it.

'This way,' Connor snarled.

They walked through a set of double doors and into a room that was at least thirty metres long and ten wide.

There were several high-backed chairs surround-
ing a fireplace, and at the far end of the room were
two antique desks pushed together. On them were
five monitors connected to computers.

The images showed various news channels and
CCTV footage of both the outside and inside of the
palace.

So far, it seemed, no one had spotted Obi's looped
recordings.

'We have a guest,' Connor said, as they approached
the chairs around the fireplace.

Hector rose from one of them.

'Hello, Jack,' he said in mock surprise. He gestured. 'Take a seat. You look like a...' he smiled,
'drowned sewer rat.'

Dripping water on the floor, Jack sat down with a
squelch.

Hector looked him up and down, and his stupid
grin spread further across his smug face.

Jack ignored him and appreciated the satisfying
warmth of the fire. Then his eyes drifted to his left.

In the third chair was Hector's father, Benito Del
Sarto. Despite heavy scars on his neck and arms, he
looked as though he was back to full health.

Del Sarto watched Jack through narrowed eyes.

'The boy had these on him.' Connor dropped the phone and objects he'd taken from Jack's pockets on to a side table and then stood back.

'You've been busy,' Hector said to Jack, sitting in the remaining chair. 'Running all over London like a homeless dog.' He clicked his fingers. 'Oh, that's right, you're homeless now, aren't you?'

Jack sighed. He couldn't be bothered with Hector's stupid games any more. All Hector wanted to do was talk, and Jack was bored with his self-satisfied droning.

Jack was about to tell him so, when a door opened and footsteps approached.

He turned in his chair to see the Shepherd walk-ing towards them.

Jack stared at him. 'So, you're in on it too.'

'You don't sound surprised,' the Shepherd said.

'No,' Jack said. 'I'm not. But I'll admit I wasn't completely sure, even though it does make perfect sense. Hector needed someone with high-level gov-ernment clearance to do what he did at the Facility. You were my number-one suspect.'

'Really?'

Jack coughed and wiped his mouth on his sleeve. 'Let me guess,' he continued, 'you used the Cer-berus forum to contact Hector, like you did us?'

The Shepherd smiled. 'You're cleverer than you look.'

'No, he's not,' Hector snapped. 'I'll prove it.'

He leapt to his feet, marched to the side table and examined the objects from Jack's pockets.

After a minute, Hector turned back. 'You want to know Jack's plan?'

'I do,' the Shepherd said, crossing his arms and leaning against the wall.

Hector smirked. 'It's pathetic.' He looked at Jack. 'He used almost the exact same tactic before in New York.'

'And what was that?' the Shepherd asked, looking genuinely intrigued.

Hector waved a finger at Jack. 'He deliberately got caught so we'd bring him inside.'

Jack shrugged and another wave of dizziness washed over him. He forced himself to focus on Hector. 'It worked though.'

The Shepherd frowned. 'I don't follow.'

'That's why he's here,' Hector said. 'He knows that he and his little friends don't stand a chance of breaking in here. So his plan is for us to bring him in ourselves, and then he'll break out instead.' He glared at Jack. 'I know you've looped the CCTV recordings. And I don't fall for the same thing twice.' Hector glanced around at everyone. 'Don't you see? I bet that girl is outside waiting for him right now.'

'She's dead,' Connor said.

Hector snorted. 'You're stupid.' He marched over to Jack, grabbed the collar of his shirt and tugged it down, revealing the modified wetsuit underneath.

Connor's eyebrows pulled together.

Hector released Jack and stepped back, turning to Connor. 'They deliberately made it look like it was an accident, you idiot, so you'd think she's not coming back. How could a dead girl be a threat to us, right? Moron.' Hector spun to face Jack again. 'And you knew that ramming the gates wouldn't get you anywhere either, so why did you do it?'

'He wanted to be chased,' Del Sarto said.

Jack glanced at him and shuffled in his chair.

'Exactly,' Hector snapped, not taking his eyes off Jack. 'You just wanted this moron to chase you.'

'Distraction,' Del Sarto said.

'That too,' Hector said. 'You wanted us to be focused on what you were doing, so your friends could pick a lock on one of the back doors, allowing you the chance to escape when you're ready.' Hector gestured to a guard. 'Go check the back of the palace.

You'll find a door unlocked. Anyone goes near it, kill them. And put the word out that there's a hole in the back fence somewhere. Send as many spare men as you can and kill anyone you find there too.'

The guard nodded and stepped from the room.

'I'm not impressed, Jack,' Hector said, rounding on him again.

'Sorry to disappoint you,' Jack croaked.

Hector shook his head. 'Not much of a plan, was it? You got over the back fence, hacked into the CCTV, then rammed the front gates.' He gestured to Connor. 'You made him chase you like a greyhound after a hare.' He paced. 'Meanwhile, your little buddies are picking the lock on a back door.' Hector sighed. 'You then fake the girl's death, and get caught. We bring you inside and you attempt to steal the antidote and get back out again.'

'I don't get it,' Connor said in a low voice.

'You don't need to get it,' Hector snarled.

He walked back to the side table, looked over the items from Jack's pockets and picked up the modified catapult. He examined it a moment, then set it down and grabbed a silver canister, forty centimetres long by ten wide. He started unscrewing the end.

'Careful with that,' Connor said.

Hector ignored him, removed the end of the canister and reached inside. He pulled out a sheet of plastic connected to a bundle of cords.

'What's that?' the Shepherd asked.

'Parachute,' Hector said. 'He thought he could get the antidote, load it into this canister and use the catapult to fire it over the wall so his friends could scoop it up.'

'Why do it that way?' Connor asked.

Hector placed the objects back on the table and chuckled. 'Because he thinks he's a hero. It's a backup plan in case he couldn't make it out of here. That way, he'd still get the antidote to them. What was it, Jack? Plan B?'

Hector dropped into the chair again. He glanced at his father with a self-satisfied smirk, then looked at Jack. 'It's a rubbish plan,' he said. 'It really is. But, to put your mind at ease, it never would've worked anyway because I've got some really bad news for you.' Hector leant forward and whispered, 'There is no antidote.'

'What?'

'You heard him,' Del Sarto snarled.

Hector sat back and laughed. 'There never has been an antidote.'

Jack's gaze moved to the Shepherd. He was smiling too.

'I deleted all records pertaining to the Medusa virus, including the antidote formula,' the Shepherd said.

'The Repository,' Jack said in a quiet voice. 'That's how you found my USB drive. You went to the Repository and destroyed every file to do with Medusa.'

'Yes,' the Shepherd said, straightening his tie. 'That's correct. Hector's men took care of everyone who knew about Medusa when they raided the Facility. Everyone who had the knowledge to create an antidote is dead.'

'But why?' Jack said. 'What's in it for you?'

'A share,' Hector said. 'A very large share of everything we've taken.' He smirked. 'Not to mention guaranteed safe passage from the country and a small island somewhere.'

Jack slumped in his chair.

Hector laughed. 'We've played you since day one. The virus was only infectious for an hour after you were exposed to it.'

Jack nodded. His suspicions had been right on that score. But his thoughts drifted back to the Facility and when he'd opened that canister. As he'd made his way out of the underground building, the only people he'd come into direct contact with were Charlie, Obi, Slink and Wren. He'd also been right about Raze, Wilf and Domino – it had taken the Outlaws longer than an hour to get back to them.

'I lied to you,' the Shepherd said. 'None of us is immunised, because none of us needs to be. Medusa was designed to only last one hour – giving it time to infect the enemy it was unleashed on and causing minimal collateral damage.'

Hector laughed. 'That's the brilliance of my plan, Jack. The Shepherd destroyed all records and eliminated all personnel who knew about the Medusa virus. Then –'

'The government thought Medusa would spread like any other virus,' Jack finished. 'They assumed everyone would become infected.'

Hector rubbed his hands together. 'Just to prove you had the virus, we sent you into quarantine for a little while.'

'We tested your blood when you were unconscious,' the Shepherd added.

'And once you'd shown the results to the right people, you deliberately let us escape,' Jack said. 'So we could be seen spreading the virus around London and also speed up the evacuation.'

Hector took a deep breath. 'So, no virus, no anti-dote,' he said. 'Only you and your pathetic "Urban Outlaws" will die.'

'Meantime, London is held to ransom,' Jack said.

'And we're free to take whatever we want,' Hector continued. 'All the while, the government are left scratching their heads and thanking their lucky stars the virus didn't spread.'

Jack glanced at the Shepherd then back to Hector, who was grinning from ear to ear, like an annoying clown.

And that's exactly what Hector is – a clown, Jack thought. *Just like his father.*

'Plan C,' he breathed.

'What did you say?'

Jack cleared his throat. 'I said, it's time for Plan C.'

The grin slipped from Hector's face. He looked over at Connor. 'Go outside,' he said. 'Round up the other Outlaws. They'll be waiting for our hero.'

Connor went to leave.

'No, they won't,' Jack called after him.

Connor stopped and turned back.

Jack rubbed his stinging eyes. He just needed to stay awake for a little while longer. 'I told them to meet me far away from here,' he said.

Hector frowned. 'What do you mean?'

'I lied.' Jack looked at him. 'I lied to them,' he croaked. 'They trust me and I said that I'd meet them at another location. I wanted them as far away from the palace as possible.'

Hector glanced at his father and back to Jack. 'Why would you do that?'

'It's another trick,' Del Sarto growled.

'No more tricks,' Jack said, slumping further in his chair and fighting to stay conscious. 'I'm tired of them. They wear me out almost as much as this virus does.' He looked at Hector. 'I knew you'd be expecting more tricks.' He nodded at the objects on the table. 'That's why I asked Charlie to make all of those. I wasn't planning to use any of them. I just needed information from you before I decided which plan to use.'

Hector's eyes narrowed.

Jack looked at the Shepherd next. 'I also know you didn't destroy the formula for the antidote.'

All eyes moved to the Shepherd, but he didn't react.

'What is he on about?' Hector said.

'He didn't destroy the formula,' Jack repeated, as if talking to a five-year-old. 'Because that would be

295

a very, very stupid thing to do. A mistake you'd make, Hector, but not him.'

Hector rose from his chair, his gaze locked on the Shepherd. 'Is this true?'

The Shepherd hesitated, and then gave a single nod.

'Why?' Hector growled.

'Hector.' Jack raised a hand and clicked his fingers. 'Focus.'

Hector spun back to face him.

'Let's see if you can follow this,' Jack said, enjoying being the smug one for a change. 'The Shepherd wanted insurance. He knew that if all this went wrong then he'd need leverage. If you were caught, he'd exchange the antidote, curing us for his freedom.' Jack looked over at Del Sarto Senior and sighed. 'You really shouldn't have let Hector run the show.' He coughed. 'Your boy has messed up, big time.'

'No, I haven't.' Hector waved a finger at the Shepherd. 'So what if he has the antidote? I don't care. It makes no difference to my plans.'

Jack's vision tunnelled. He blinked, dragging his mind back to the present moment, and tried to sit up straight. 'It's over, Hector.'

'It's not over,' Hector snapped. 'I told you it makes no difference, and whatever you say next, I'm not falling for another one of your tricks. We carry on as planned.'

'Yeah, I did say no more tricks, didn't I?' Jack said. 'Well, I lied about that too.' He put a hand under the wetsuit. 'But this is definitely the last one. I promise.' He pulled out Abdul's mobile phone, which was wrapped in a clear waterproof bag and connected to a microphone. Jack tossed it on to the rug at their feet.

Hector stared down at it. The display showed that a call to Noble was in progress.

Thanks to Noble handing himself in to the authorities and explaining the situation to them, they would have heard everything Hector and the Shepherd had just said about their plans and still having the formula to the antidote.

Check.

Mate.

'The boy sacrificed himself,' the Shepherd said in barely a whisper.

Jack couldn't tell if it was surprise or admiration in his voice.

'I reckon you've got about ten minutes to get out of here,' Jack said.

He slumped in the chair again, as exhaustion threatened to overwhelm him.

That was his final play – he had no more left.

Jack sat back and hoped that he stayed alive long enough to watch the events unfold, knowing his friends were saved.

Besides, he wanted to enjoy this.

For several seconds, everyone looked at each other.

Suddenly, Hector erupted, lunged forwards and grabbed Jack by the throat. 'I'm going to kill you,' he roared.

'I'll do it.' Del Sarto stood, raising a gun. 'Stand back.'

Hector let go of Jack and stepped aside.

Del Sarto pointed the gun at Jack's head. 'I should've done this when I had the chance.'

Jack closed his eyes.

There was a clicking sound.

'I wouldn't do that, if I were you.'

Jack opened his eyes to see the Shepherd was pressing his own gun against Del Sarto's temple.

'What are you doing?' Hector screamed.

'Protecting my leverage,' the Shepherd said. 'You kill the boy, you'll ruin my chances at getting out of this.'

Connor drew his weapon and aimed it at the Shepherd.

The Shepherd glanced at Connor. 'It's time to choose a side.'

The remaining guard stepped forward, a finger pressed to his ear. 'Sir, snipers report helicopters heading this way.'

'Not much time left,' the Shepherd said to Connor. 'What's your decision? Come with me and you might stand a chance.'

Connor hesitated, then swung his gun to face Del Sarto.

Hector's eyes went wide. 'What are you doing?'

'I suggest you lower your weapon,' the Shepherd said.

Del Sarto's face twisted with rage and his finger tightened on the trigger.

Jack braced himself.

For a few seconds, no one moved, then Del Sarto roared and threw his gun across the room.

'Dad,' Hector shouted. 'What are you doing?'

'Shut up,' he snarled.

Jack let out a breath.

'Wise choice.' The Shepherd pulled Jack from the chair and half-carried him towards the door.

Connor, his gun still raised, went with them.

'You're not going to get away with this,' Hector growled.

The Shepherd gave a slight shrug. 'We'll see.'

They burst through the doors and hurried to the SUV.

The Shepherd flung open the rear door and threw Jack on to the back seat, while Connor climbed into the front.

'Go,' the Shepherd shouted.

Connor did a wheelspin across the forecourt, through the archway and towards the gates.

The guard at the gates turned to face them with a puzzled expression.

Connor wound down his window. 'Open the gates and run.' He pointed at three helicopters as they approached.

The guard hesitated, then did as he was told.

Connor rammed his foot to the floor and they raced down the Mall.

Jack felt himself slipping away and he focused all his remaining energy to stay conscious.

'Where are we going?' Connor said over his shoulder to the Shepherd.

'City Hall.'

A couple of minutes later, they were driving alongside the Thames.

Jack glanced over at the river and hoped that Charlie had got out safely. He also vaguely wondered if the Outlaws were still waiting for him at the rendezvous point. Surely they would have seen the helicopters moving in on the palace by now?

Suddenly, the rear window of the SUV exploded, showering Jack and the Shepherd in glass.

Jack glanced back to see the Rolls-Royce in pursuit, with Hector hanging out of the passenger window, aiming a gun at them.

Hector fired again and the bullets thudded into the ceiling above Jack's head.

The Shepherd shoved him down on to the seat and returned fire.

The sound of his gun inside the confined space was deafening, sending a sharp pain through Jack's eardrums.

The SUV wove violently from side to side then screeched around the corner.

Jack glanced up to see that they were speeding across Tower Bridge.

The next second, there was a loud *bang*. The SUV jolted to the left and was suddenly rolling over sideways.

Jack covered his head with his arms as his world tumbled end over end, slamming him into the seats and ceiling.

Finally, the SUV stopped spinning and Jack opened his eyes again. It was now on its roof and the Shepherd was hanging from his seat belt, unconscious, like a rag doll.

Connor groaned from the front seat and was trying in vain to release his legs from under the steering wheel.

Jack undid his own belt and dragged himself out through the side window, over broken glass and debris.

A bolt of pain shot through his leg and he looked down to see it was soaked in blood.

He rolled on to his back, breathing heavily, his vision tunnelling again.

A pair of car doors opened and closed.

Dazed, Jack craned his neck back and watched as two pairs of shoes strode towards him. Hector and his father.

Suddenly, a helicopter thundered overhead, making them stop dead in their tracks.

A loud voice boomed over a loudspeaker, 'Drop your weapons on the ground and put your hands up.'

Jack's body went limp and his world faded to black.

CHAPTER FIFTEEN

LIGHT PIERCED THROUGH THE DARKNESS. JACK groaned, opened his eyes and was greeted by Charlie's face staring down at him.

She was wearing a hospital gown under a bathrobe.

Jack blinked a few times and glanced around. He was lying in bed in a private hospital room. His leg was bandaged and there was an intravenous drip connected to his arm.

He looked back at Charlie. 'I'm alive?'

She punched him.

'*Ow*. What was that for?'

'For lying to us.' After a second, Charlie's face softened and she bent down and hugged him. 'We thought we'd lost you.'

It was then that Jack saw Obi, Slink and Wren standing by the door and, despite all being dressed in hospital gowns too, they looked fit and healthy.

Thank God they were all safe.

Charlie straightened up and wiped tears from her face.

'How long have I been asleep?' Jack asked her.

'Three days.'

'And I assume from the fact we're all here that the Shepherd handed over the formula for the antidote?'

'Yeah.' Charlie smiled. 'It was a very close call though.'

'Are you going to explain what happened?' Slink said. 'Or have we gotta get Charlie to beat it out of ya?'

Jack winced as he tried to prop his head up with a pillow. His whole body was stiff and there wasn't a part of him that didn't hurt like crazy. 'There's not much to tell you.'

'Yeah, right,' Obi said.

'You went rogue on us,' Wren said. 'And you told *me* off for doing that before.'

Jack grimaced. 'You're right. I'm sorry. I won't do it again.'

'Come on then,' Obi said. 'What happened?'

Jack sighed. 'I was tired. I wasn't really thinking straight and felt awful, like you all did. No matter what I tried to think of, I couldn't come up with a plan to beat Hector. Plus I couldn't be sure where the antidote was or –'

'If he even had it,' Charlie finished.

'Yeah,' Jack said. 'I couldn't be sure about anything. But when I really thought about it, some things fell into place. Like the fact that the Shepherd was in on it. And if the Shepherd was working with the Del Sartos, he was clever enough to have some kind of insurance. A way to protect himself should Hector's plans not pan out.'

'But how did you know he had the antidote?' Slink asked.

'Because he told me.'

'Huh?' Charlie said. 'When?'

'Not deliberately,' Jack said. 'At least, I don't think so. He gave me my USB drive back, the one I'd left at the Repository, which told me he'd been there.'

'To destroy the antidote records,' Obi said.

Jack half-smiled. 'If you'd been ordered to destroy those records, would you have done it?'

'I would've made a copy,' Slink said. 'Just in case I needed –'

'Leverage,' Jack said. 'Exactly.'

'But you still couldn't be totally sure the Shepherd had the antidote formula,' said Wren.

'No,' Jack said, 'I couldn't. I needed proof.'

'So, what did you do?' Obi asked.

'I needed a confession. But I also knew that Hector would be expecting all of our tricks. He'd be prepared for everything we threw at him. I decided to do exactly that – give him what he was expecting. I made it look like we were following a mission, when in fact –'

'You were sacrificing yourself,' Charlie said.

Jack shrugged. 'It was a huge gamble, but the most important thing was for the government to know everything. Then, no matter what happened to me, you guys would get the antidote one way or another.'

'I can't believe you were giving up your own life for ours,' Wren said in barely a whisper.

'You make it sound noble,' Jack said. 'I was just protecting my family, that's all. I know you guys would've done the same for me.' He glanced around. 'Speaking of Noble, is he OK?'

'He's perfectly fine.' Noble strode into the room with a huge grin on his face.

Jack let out a breath, relieved he was all right.

'What happened to Hector and his dad?' Jack asked.

Noble pursed his lips. 'Do you remember what the Facility was used for before it was turned into those laboratories and storage?'

Jack chuckled. 'Yeah. A top-secret prison.'

Noble's smile broadened. 'It seems that the Del Sartos are going to be in a similar prison for a very long time.'

Jack let out a huge sigh, relieved it was finally over.

'Well,' Slink said, slapping his hands together and looking round at them all, 'I can't wait for our next mission. It's gonna be –'

'Relaxing,' Jack said, slumping back on to the pillows. 'Something really, really easy.'

Now all of them were grinning at him.

Two weeks later, Jack, Charlie, Obi and Wren were sitting on a wall overlooking the newly built skate and parkour park. It was in an empty lot between two buildings, and had been a joint RAKing venture between the Outlaws, Raze, Wilf and Domino.

In front of them was a granite block with a brass plaque that read, *Dedicated to Scarlett. The bravest girl that ever lived.*

Jack's eyes roamed over the park. It seemed as though virtually every kid in London was there – some were on skateboards, others on Rollerblades, while several kids were clambering up and over bars and jumping off walls.

Jack spotted Ryan at the other end of the park. He was on a bike, pulling wheelies and doing tricks, with a group of onlookers.

Jack couldn't help but beam at it all.

Charlie looked at him. 'What's with you?'

'It's just...' He shrugged. 'This is what we're supposed to do, you know? This is what being an Urban Outlaw means to me – doing RAKing missions, helping other people. Making them happy. Putting smiles on faces.'

'And making sure bad people get their comeuppance, while we're at it,' Wren said.

'Yeah, that too. Speaking of which...' Jack put a hand into his pocket and pulled out three sets of diamond-encrusted cufflinks and a gold watch.

They gaped at him.

'Where did you get those?' Wren asked.

'They were Hector's dad's,' Jack said. 'Talya stole them from the hotel suite, so I took them from her.' He looked at Charlie. 'You're not the only one who can pinch things from Talya's warehouse when she's not looking. Besides, you did say you wanted to donate to that clothes bank we stole from. Think this will make up for it?'

Charlie grinned.

'Jack, what happens if we come across more bad guys?' Obi said. 'We won't be able to do anything about them.'

Thanks to Hector, the Urban Outlaws were famous now. They couldn't go anywhere without people recognising them. In fact, it had got so out of control that the day before, a bunch of kids had even asked for their autographs.

Ridiculous.

'Obi's right,' Charlie said. 'If we can't do missions like we used to, what are we going to do from now on?'

Jack glanced between them all. 'Actually, I've had a really good idea about that.'

'*Guys.*' Slink came running up, looking like he was about to burst with excitement.

'What's wrong with you?' Charlie asked him.

Slink was practically hyperventilating. 'You're not gonna believe it.'

Jack frowned. 'What? Spit it out.'

Slink took several breaths and said, 'I've found the perfect new hideout for us.'

ACKNOWLEDGEMENTS

PETER JAY BLACK WOULD LIKE TO CONVEY A SPECIAL
THANK YOU TO THE FOLLOWING PEOPLE

Literary Agent	JO WILLIAMSON
Literary Agency	ANTONY HARWOOD LTD
Editorial Director	ELLEN HOLGATE
Senior Commissioning Editor	RACHEL BODEN
Managing Director	EMMA HOPKIN
Publishing Directors	REBECCA MCNALLY, CINDY LOH
Managing Editor	HELEN VICK
Executive Director	CRISTINA GILBERT
Assistant Editors	NATALIE HAMILTON, LUCY MACKAY-SIM
Editorial Assistants	HALI BAUMSTEIN, VICKY LEECH
Copy-Editors	ISABEL FORD, TALYA BAKER, MADELEINE STEVENS
Publicity	LIZZ SKELLY, IAN LAMB, CHARLOTTE HAYNES
Marketing	GRACE WHOOLEY, SONIA PALMISANO
Designers	KATIE EVERSON, MAIA FJORD
Production Controller	JENNY BEER
Rights Executive	JENNA BROWN
Audio Narrator	ANDY CRESSWELL

PETER JAY BLACK would like to THANK all of the EARLY REVIEWERS:
JACK, LEWIS, OLLIE, LUKE, SCARLETT, TOM, FRANKIE, MILO, SAM
and also WILF, RYAN and JAMES (aka THE CONSULTANT)

Thank you and my HUMBLE APPRECIATION to
LYN, KIRSTY, MARK, STEVE, BRIAN, ANN, DIANNE and MY FAMILY

With EXTRA THANKS to:
DARREN HARTWELL at BOOKS FOR BOYS
MICHELLE at MUCH LOVED BOOKS
SUE and LINDA at THE BOOK BAG
and VINCENT aka MR RIPLEY

PETER JAY BLACK would like to say an EXTRA-SPECIAL
THANK YOU to YOU, the READER ...

THE URBAN

JACK

HACKER NAME: **ACHILLES**
REAL NAME: **JACK FENTON**
AGE: **15**
SPECIAL SKILL: **HACKING**
LIKES: **PHYSICS**
DISLIKES: **DUBSTEP**
GREATEST FEAR: **HEIGHTS**

CHARLIE

HACKER NAME: **PANDORA**
REAL NAME: **CHARLOTTE CAINE**
AGE: **15**
SPECIAL SKILL: **MAKING GADGETS**
LIKES: **COMPUTER GAMES**
DISLIKES: **GROSS HABITS**
GREATEST FEAR: **FIRE**